Loch Ness Murder

A Charlie Kingsley Novella

Other books by Michele Pariza Wacek
MPWNovels.com/books

Secrets of Redemption series:
It Began With a Lie (Book 1)
This Happened to Jessica (Book 2)
The Evil That Was Done (Book 3)
The Summoning (Book 4)
The Reckoning (Book 5)
The Girl Who Wasn't There (Book 6)
The Room at the Top of the Stairs (Book 7)
The Secret Diary of Helen Blackstone (free novella)

Charlie Kingsley Mystery series:
A Grave Error (free prequel novella)
The Murder Before Christmas (Book 1)
Ice Cold Murder (Book 2)
Murder Next Door (Book 3)
Murder Among Friends (Book 4)
The Murder of Sleepy Hollow (Book 5)
Red Hot Murder (Book 6)
A Wedding to Murder For (novella)
Loch Ness Murder (novella)

Standalone books:
Today I'll See Her (novella)
The Taking
The Third Nanny
Mirror Image
The Stolen Twin

Loch Ness Murder

A Charley Kingsley Novella

by Michele Pariza Wacek

ISBN 978-1-945363-68-9

For my family, for always believing in me.

Chapter 1

"Wait, which monster did you say you wanted to document again?"

Nancy's voice floated across the lobby as I pulled open the door to the Redemption Inn, a charming bed and breakfast. It was built like a log cabin, with hardwood floors, polished oak furniture, and cozy quilts. Nancy, the owner, was one of my tea clients. She stood eying the two men standing in front of the check-in desk, her silver glasses perched on her nose.

"The ones at Angel's Lake," said the first man eagerly, dropping his bag so he could paw through a notebook he carried under his arm. He wore an ill-fitting brown suit that matched his badly cut hair and smudged glasses.

"Oh, you mean Locky," Nancy said, reaching up to adjust her hair, which was as brittle as old straw thanks to many bad perm and color jobs.

The second man blinked confusedly at her. He too was in a rumpled suit, but his was blue, and his tie was askew, as though he had been pulling on it. "'Locky'?"

"Yeah. You know how the Loch Ness Monster is called 'Nessie'? We call ours 'Locky.'"

Both men just stared at her. "That doesn't make any sense," Brown Suit said, his voice agitated. "The Loch Ness Monster is called that because it lives in a loch in Scotland that's fed by the River Ness."

Now it was Nancy's turn to return the confused blinking. "Loch? You mean a lake."

"No, I mean a loch, although it is an old Gaelic word for 'lake,'" Brown Suit said. "It's a common misconception."

"I didn't know that," Nancy said. "You really do learn something new every day."

"But that's why the name doesn't make sense," Brown Suit continued, his agitation rising. "You might as well call him 'Lakey.'"

"Um," Nancy uttered.

"And furthermore," Brown Suit continued, "this lake is called 'Angel's Lake,' not 'Loch Ness.' It doesn't make sense to name a monster after a lake it doesn't even live in." At that, he flapped his arms wildly, scattering his papers everywhere.

Nancy stared at him, clearly torn as to whether she should help him pick up his papers or just change the subject. "Um, well, you make a good point. Unfortunately, I didn't have anything to do with the naming convention of our local Loch Ness … errr … lake monster."

"It's important to accurately identify creatures, so you can refer to them by their proper name," Blue Suit said. "If you aren't calling them by their correct name, how will you know how to handle them?"

"People don't realize how many sea creatures there are," Brown Suit interjected as he awkwardly gathered his papers. "I realize this is a freshwater lake and not an ocean, but it's certainly possible something from the sea learned to adapt to fresh water."

"Precisely," Blue Suit agreed. "It may not even be a lake monster. What if it's a water nymph or sprite … or a selkie? Calling it 'Locky' would make even less sense."

"Actually, the correct term is 'naiads,' not 'water nymphs,'" Brown Suit corrected, giving Blue Suit the side-eye.

Blue Suit flushed. "I was using the term 'water nymphs' because it is more common than 'naiads,' and I wanted to make sure everyone understood." He gestured with his head toward Nancy.

"I am familiar with naiads," Nancy said drily.

"Yes, but if we're going to insist on correct naming conventions …" Brown Suit said, ignoring Nancy.

Nancy glanced away, an eye roll imminent, but that's when she saw me.

"Charlie," she said, her voice loud as she interrupted, clearly relieved by the distraction. "I'm so glad you stopped by. I'll be with you in a minute, after I check in these two gentlemen."

The aforementioned gentlemen turned to gawk at me. Both wore thick glasses, and their eyes were wide and round as they stared.

"Oh, you're a girl," Brown Suit said matter-of-factly.

"Yes, I am," I confirmed.

"With a name like 'Charlie,' I was expecting a man," he sniffed. He turned back to Nancy. "This is why naming things properly is important. Otherwise, people can make the wrong assumptions."

"Charlie can be a girl's name, too," I said.

"There are more men named 'Charlie' than women," Brown Suit said. He kept his head down, not meeting my eyes as he fussed with his papers. "It's very confusing."

The mention of my name had clearly thrown him for a loop, and rather than being upset about it, I found myself feeling sorry for him. Actually, I was feeling sorry for everyone in the situation, including Nancy, who seemed flummoxed by this particular check-in process.

"So, you're going to investigate our lake," I said.

Brown Suit glanced up, his brow furrowed, his expression a mix of confusion and distrust, but despite all of that, his eagerness to talk about his work won out.

"It's well-documented that very few bodies are recovered from Angel's Lake," he said. "Bodies don't surface in cold, deep lakes the way they do when the water is warmer and shallower. But, my research has shown that sometimes, other factors are at play."

"Other factors," I said, nodding. "Like the naiads and water nymphs and Loch Ness Monsters?"

"Naiads and water nymphs are the same thing," Brown Suit said, his tone reproachful.

"I stand corrected," I said.

"And the Loch Ness Monster isn't an actual breed," Blue Suit continued. "It's most likely a plesiosaur."

"So, you think we might have a naiad or plesiosaur in our lake?"

"We don't know what you have. That's why we're researching it," Brown Suit said.

"It's possible there's nothing going on other than the lake being cold and deep," Blue Suit added. "But we've heard the stories and think it's worth checking out."

"What stories?" I asked. Behind the men, Nancy could no longer control it—she rolled her eyes.

Redemption, Wisconsin, is a charming little town that also has a haunted past. Back in 1888, all the adults disappeared. Only the children were left, and they all swore they had no idea what happened to the adults.

Since then, Redemption had been a hotbed of strange and mysterious events. People frequently disappeared without a trace, along with other unexplained happenings. Then there's the many haunted buildings, including my own house. There were so many stories, in fact, that even though I'd been living in the town for a few years already, I'd only heard a fraction of them, and I still couldn't keep track of them all. I really needed to start keeping a record.

"Well, the stories of Angel's Lake being haunted," Brown Suit said, flipping through his notes. "There have been sightings of a variety of creatures. Lake monsters similar to the Loch Ness, beings that look like humans in the water, which could be the naiads or selkies or sprites, or maybe even some sort of fresh-water mermaid." Brown Suit's eyes gleamed from behind his glasses. "I know everyone thinks all those creatures are myths or legends, but I've discovered proof to the contrary."

"Proof?" I asked. "What sort of proof?"

Brown Suit's eyes went wide with horror. "Oh! I can't tell you that." He hugged his notes to his chest and took a step backward, as if I was about to leap forward and pry them from his arms. "It's very confidential."

"That's why we're here," Blue Suit said. "We're going to be publishing our findings soon, and we're hoping Angel's Lake will give us the final data points we need before we release it all to the world."

"What we've discovered is going to be earth-shattering," Brown Suit said. "It's going to set the scientific establishment on its head. So, we need to make sure we dot all our I's and cross our T's."

Blue Suit nodded solemnly. "We need to be prepared. It's going to be like opening Pandora's box. Once it happens, it's going to blow a lot of people's minds. So, we need irrefutable proof."

"Which we have," Brown Suit was quick to add. "But it can't hurt to have more."

"Wow, 'irrefutable proof,'" I repeated. I couldn't imagine what that could be. Photographs? Those could be doctored. Same as recordings. But whatever it was, they seemed extremely confident it would hold up to the scrutiny of the scientific community. "I'll be interested in seeing it."

"You won't be disappointed," Brown Suit assured me.

"Well, if that's the case, I hope you find what you're looking for in our little lake," I said.

From behind them, I saw Nancy roll her eyes again.

Chapter 2

"I wish we could have talked Claire into joining us," Pat said as we plodded through the sand.

Pat was my best friend, as well as one of my first tea clients. "Don't go too far," she called out to Daphne, Claire's toddler, as she ran happily ahead. "I forgot how exhausting a two-year-old can be," she said as she adjusted her round sunglasses on her face. Everything about Pat was round—round body, round hair, round glasses, or in this case, sunglasses. With her other hand, she pulled her large hat more firmly onto her head.

Claire was my other best friend, and the first person I met when I arrived in Redemption. Something had shifted with her after she got pregnant with Daphne, and she hadn't been the same. I wasn't completely sure why, as she didn't like to talk about it, but I had my suspicions.

Claire had good days and bad days, and this was a bad one.

"I agree. The sun and fresh air would have probably done her a lot of good," I said as I trudged alongside Pat, struggling to carry the umbrella, food, towels, and toys for Daphne. I wasn't entirely sure how I ended up carrying everything, while Pat only seemed to have one task at hand—keeping her hat on her head. *Although, maybe she has the right idea,* I thought as another gust of wind blew my hair across my face. I inwardly groaned thinking of the combing experience I was bound to be up against later. My hair, a wild, curly mass of brownish-blond-ish- reddish locks, was high maintenance under normal circumstances. And these weren't normal.

"Not to mention we wouldn't be in charge of the two-year-old," Pat said. When we'd gone to Claire's to invite her, Daphne had been so excited at the thought that none of us wanted to disappoint her. So, we ended up agreeing to take Daphne and leave Claire to rest at home. Even though the thought of being in charge of an active two-year-old was daunting, once we were there, it was hard to doubt we hadn't made the right choice. It was a perfect day for a trip to the beach, with the sun shining brightly and a brisk breeze to keep it from feeling too hot.

"She's a handful," I said, watching Daphne tumble forward onto the sand and laugh hysterically. "I don't know ... maybe it's for the best. Maybe Claire needs a break even more than fresh air and sunshine."

Pat yanked on her hat. "We probably ought to offer to take Daphne off of Claire's hands more."

"It sure couldn't hurt." I knew Claire wasn't keen on leaving Daphne alone with just anyone. Plus, Daphne was picky. If she liked you, she was extremely easygoing, but if she didn't ... well, it could get ugly pretty fast. Amelia, Claire's sister, learned that lesson the hard way. Unfortunately for Claire, it made her reluctant to leave Daphne with anyone new.

"Daphne, not so fast," Pat called out again. "Oh, that child. Here. Let's set up here, and I'll go catch her before she runs straight into the lake."

I dropped everything into the sand, taking a moment to roll my shoulders back as Pat went chasing after Daphne, who looked like she was having the time of her life. By the time Pat corralled her, I had the umbrella up, the towels down, and Daphne's sand toys laid out invitingly. I even filled the pail with lake water. Daphne's face lit up when she saw the display, and she immediately settled down and started digging.

Pat collapsed on her towel. "I'm too old for this," she groaned.

I hid a grin as I dug a Coke out of the cooler. "This will help."

"A cookie would help more," she said as she took her drink.

"You want a cookie now, or do you want to wait until after we eat our sandwiches?"

Pat eyed me over her sunglasses. "What do you think?"

I began digging for one of my famous chocolate chip cookies, keeping an eye on Daphne in case she saw what I was doing and wanted one, as well. Engrossed in her sandcastle, she was too distracted to notice.

I handed Pat her cookie and leaned back on my elbows, gazing at the variety of kids and adults playing in Angel's Lake.

It was like a sparkling jewel, brilliant in the sunshine, making it nearly impossible to imagine any sort of sea monster lurking in its depths.

"So, what's the story with this lake?" I asked Pat.

She took a swig of Coke, making a slight face as she had just eaten half her cookie. "What do you want to know?"

"Is there really a monster named 'Lakey' living in it?"

"You mean 'Locky'?"

"Oh, yeah. That's right. Locky. I got confused, because apparently, 'loch' is another name for 'lake.'"

Pat turned to look at me. "Really? I didn't know that. So, the Loch Ness Monster is actually living in a lake called 'Ness'?"

"Apparently."

"Well, that explains why they named it 'Nessie,'" Pat mused. "How did you find this out?"

"Oh, from these two guys who are apparently here investigating all the strange stuff that's happened in the lake." I gave her a brief rundown of what occurred at the Redemption Inn.

"You know, with all the unexplained things that have happened here over the years, I can't believe it's taken this long for someone to come check it out," Pat said.

"Yeah, you'd think this place would be crawling with ghost hunters," I agreed.

"I suppose that means Redemption didn't want to be investigated," Pat mused. "I wonder what's changed now."

Along with all the other weird things that had taken place in Redemption, the townspeople were convinced that it—the town itself—decided who stayed and who left. Never mind that it made no sense ... that a town could make conscious decisions or have anything to do with that. Nonetheless, everyone was convinced. I had given up arguing about it, especially since I had no good reason for the bizarre series of events that resulted in my ending up a resident. From getting lost as I ran from an abusive fiancé to finding myself with a home and business selling tea, my entire life changed in about three months' time. Even I had trouble wrapping my head around it all.

"Maybe Locky is ready for primetime," I said.

Pat frowned as she considered it. "Possible. Although personally, I've never put much stake in our having our very own Loch Ness Monster. I thought it was far more realistic that it's some sort of evil water nymph."

"It's not a 'nymph'; it's a 'naiad,'" I clarified. "Accurate names are important."

Pat smirked at me. "Says the girl with a boy's name."

"Precisely," I said. "And portraying monsters correctly is equally important, Pat. Tell me, why on Earth would you think an evil naiad being in the lake is more realistic than a dinosaur?"

"Well, if we're going for accuracy here, we don't actually know if the Loch Ness Monster is a dinosaur," Pat said. "But putting that aside, I'm skeptical of Locky existing mainly because he's way too big. How could none of us have seen something that huge in this lake by now?" She waved her hand toward the water. "And is there enough food in there to feed it? Naiads are much smaller, and I suspect they don't eat as much, if at all. So that's why I think it's more likely to be a naiad. Plus, I have a friend who saw it."

I choked on my Coke. "Your friend saw it?"

"Yeah, Bridget. You met Bridget, right? It was a number of years ago. She had gone swimming in the lake at night, and something grabbed her leg and pulled her under."

I sat up. "Really?"

Pat nodded. "Yeah. Later, everyone said it was probably just seaweed, but she insisted she actually felt it grab her. Like a hand with claws. She apparently had claw marks on her calf."

I shivered, despite the heat of the sun. "Claw marks?"

"Yeah. Her calf was really scraped up."

"So, then what happened?"

"Well, she got pulled under and was kicking and thrashing to get away. She thought she was caught in the weeds as well, because she looked down and saw all these strands floating around her. But then they parted, and these two green eyes opened and were staring right at her. That's when she realized what she thought was weeds … was hair."

Just then, a gust of wind whipped through my own hair, causing goosebumps to rise on the back of my neck. I could smell the lake, slightly fishy and algae-like, and I suddenly thought our day trip maybe wasn't such a good idea. "There were eyes staring at her? In the water?"

"Freaky, huh?"

"How did she get away?"

"One of her friends grabbed her."

"One of her friends? Wait a second … she wasn't alone? But no one saw anything?"

Pat's mouth quirked up in a sardonic grin. "I think I left out the part that she had been drinking. She had just graduated from college, and they had a big party by the Rock. It was an unseasonably hot night, so she and a few friends decided to skinny dip. Bridget used to love swimming, so she was the first in. Anyway, that was when it happened. Her friend who pulled her out thought she was drowning. Needless to say, no one believed her about the eyes."

"What about the claw marks on her leg?"

"Well, remember she had come from partying at the Rock. There's a lot of trees and branches around there. People assumed she scraped herself there and didn't realize it."

I sat back on my towel, making sure Daphne was still building her sandcastle. "Wow. That's quite a story."

"Yeah." Pat settled back, as well. "It's not the only one out there, either. There have been several people I can think of off the top of my head who have had similar experiences. They all claim it was some sort of water nymph … errr … 'naiad,' that tried to drown them."

"Does the naiad have a name?"

"Oh, heaven's no." Pat shook her head emphatically. "That would be like trying to attract its attention, and trust me, no one wants that."

"But 'Locky' is fine," I said sarcastically.

"Well, of course." Pat shot me a look that clearly implied a "duh." "Who would you rather run into, a swimming dinosaur, or a murderous naiad? Besides, Nessie hasn't killed anyone. At least not to my knowledge."

"When you put it that way, the swimming dinosaur wins out," I said. "So, do people have Locky stories, as well?"

"What do you think? It's Redemption. It wouldn't be Redemption if we didn't have stories about multiple lake entities prowling around. But compared to the murderous naiad, Locky sightings are pretty tame. They're usually far off in the distance, like across the lake, and they don't last long. There's even been the occasional picture, but they're usually fuzzy and out of focus, so they could be anything, really. Anyway, I don't know when Locky officially got his name. He's had it for as long as I can remember."

"I take it you've never seen Locky," I said.

"Nah. Although to be fair, I haven't been looking, either. I'm not too keen on seeing either resident of the lake." Pat shivered. "I have enough ghosts and goblins and other assorted monsters to deal with on Redemption's land. I don't need to add lake monsters into the mix. However, I do know people who have seen Locky."

Daphne chose that moment to pick up her empty bucket, and after glancing around, suddenly take off toward the lake.

"Daphne, no! Not the lake," Pat yelled as I leapt to my feet.

"My turn to get her," I said, and I took off running after the toddler, who was already closer to the lake than I was comfortable with. I was always amazed at how fast those little legs could run.

The sand was hot under my feet, and it felt like I was moving in slow motion. Pat was hollering at Daphne, which was good, because I was able to conserve my breath for running.

I caught up with her right at the edge of the water, as a wave gently lapped over her feet. She giggled.

"Daphne, remember what we talked about," I said, trying to catch my breath while inwardly making a note to get back to step class. "You can only go into the water with an adult."

"Wah-ter," Daphne said, holding up her bucket.

"Yeah, so we're clear?" I asked, taking the bucket. "No more water, unless one of us is with you."

"Wah-ter," Daphne said again and pointed to the bucket.

I sighed and waded in a little deeper to fill her bucket, glad I had worn my swimsuit underneath an oversized tunic. Daphne followed me for a couple of steps, but the moment a bigger wave hit her, she ran screaming and giggling back to dry land.

I was busy filling her bucket when a movement near the shore caught the corner of my eye. I straightened up, shielding my eyes. Yes, there was something there, flailing by the edge of the water.

I felt my skin crawl as I quickly moved back to shore. No, it couldn't possibly be a murderous naiad. Nor could it be Locky, as it was way too small.

Whatever it was, it was certainly floundering around. Was it a person? Someone in trouble?

I snatched up Daphne and ran toward Pat, who must have seen my face, because she got to her feet and hurried to meet me. "Here," I said, thrusting Daphne at her. "I think someone is drowning over there."

Pat's eyes went wide. "Drowning? But that's not even a des-ignated swimming area." I didn't answer, as I was already run-ning over.

I could hear Pat call for more help behind me as I dashed over to the figure and waded in. From what I could tell, it was a man wearing a short-sleeve button-down shirt. A part of me wondered why someone would be swimming so close to shore while fully dressed, but that thought disappeared as I focused on getting out to him as quickly as I could.

Luckily, he wasn't that far out. In fact, it wasn't even that deep where he was—I could touch the bottom.

"It's okay," I shouted, grabbing the man's arm. "You can touch the bottom. Just relax. Put your feet down."

He was so panicked, he nearly slugged me in the face, but I kept talking to him in a soothing voice. Soon, he calmed down enough to realize for himself that he could stand.

I heard splashing from behind me as a couple of men ran into the water to help. "I think we're okay," I said as I started guiding the man back in to shore.

"You sure?" one of the rescuers asked, popping up next to me. He was probably in his early twenties and seemed quite fit. His dark hair hung dripping in his eyes, and he slicked it back.

"Don't leave me," the flailing man gurgled.

"No one is leaving you," I said as the other rescuer swam to his other side to support that arm. "I've got you, buddy," he said. "We're almost there."

The man we were rescuing seemed familiar, but it wasn't until we were nearly back on shore that I realized where I had seen him before.

He was Blue Suit.

I immediately started looking around, wondering where Brown Suit was, and felt an unpleasant knot in my stomach start to form.

Blue Suit was alone.

He had almost drowned, and his friend was nowhere in sight.

This wasn't boding well.

The moment Blue Suit made it to shore, he collapsed face-first onto the rocky ground, coughing and retching. A small crowd of people had started to form, including Pat. Daphne, safe in her arms, held a cookie in her hand.

I looked back to Blue Suit, who was also wearing a pair of khakis and dress shoes along with the button-down.

"Dress shoes," the rescuer said as he noticed the same. Peering down at Blue Suit, he shook his head. "No wonder he had so much trouble in the water. Buddy, you have to kick off the shoes."

Blue Suit sputtered. "These are my good shoes. Do you know what they cost me?"

"I don't think that matters anymore," the rescuer said. "They look pretty trashed to me."

Blue Suit groaned.

I knelt down next to him, trying to avoid the bigger, pointier rocks. If he had been able to manage a few more steps, we would have been on grass, but I was in no position to complain. I wasn't the one who had almost drowned. "We should probably get you to the hospital," I suggested. "Just so they can check you out."

He coughed again and looked at me, squinting. His glasses were askew and slicked with water. "Do I know you?"

I smiled. "Yeah, we met when you were checking in to the Redemption Inn. I'm Charlie."

"Charlie," he said. He spat out a mouthful of water and rolled over to a sitting position. "I remember you."

"What's your name?" I asked, when it was clear he had no intention of volunteering it.

He didn't answer right away, instead sucking in a deep breath. I was happy to see the color returning to his face, but I still thought he should see a doctor. "Stan."

"Nice to meet you, Stan," I said. "Do you know where your friend is?"

He closed his eyes, shaking his head violently. The knot in my stomach grew tighter.

"There's someone else?" the other rescuer asked, his voice alarmed. All he wore was a skimpy, turquoise-red-black bathing suit, which showed off his muscular body. He half-turned, as though ready to jump back into the lake to start searching for the missing friend.

"Don't bother," Stan said, his voice miserable. "I think it's too late."

My eyes widened. "Too late? What do you mean?"

"I think Nevin is already gone."

"Gone? You mean he's still out there?" Skimpy Bathing Suit was already on his way back down to the shore.

"No," Stan called out again. "It's too late."

"How do you know that?" Skimpy Bathing Suit asked.

"Because he went out on the lake last night and didn't come back," Stan said.

Skimpy Bathing Suit paused to stare at Stan. "He went out on the lake?"

"Stan, I think you better start from the beginning," I prompted.

Stan nodded and coughed again. "We had a breakthrough with our research yesterday. Around what you would consider your Loch Ness Monster."

"Locky?" Skimpy Bathing Suit asked. "You saw Locky?"

"More than that," Stan said. "We discovered undeniable proof of his existence."

There it was again ... that notion of "undeniable" proof. What on Earth could it be? "Really?" I asked.

He nodded, his eyes faintly lit with excitement. "But Nevin wanted to check the data. We have to be sure we've triple checked every detail, you see."

"Yes, I know," I said. "You want to make sure you're prepared for the scientific community."

Stan beamed. "Yes, exactly." Then, he frowned. "I told Nevin to wait until the morning. I told him it wasn't safe to be on the lake at night, but he insisted. He didn't come home last night, so this morning, I went looking for him. I didn't find him, but I did find our boat."

"Where was it?" I asked.

"It was drifting. Out there." Stan waved his hand toward the lake.

Skimpy Bathing Suit turned to look at the lake. "It was just drifting out there? No one in it?"

Stan shook his head. "No, it was empty."

"What did you do? Did you call the cops?" I asked.

"No, I thought I should go get my boat first, in case there was anything in it that would help me find him. Or, maybe he was even still in it, but lying down, or something. So, I hired someone to take me out there and bring the boat back in."

"Who did you hire?" Skimpy Bathing Suit asked.

Stan squished up his face. "Someone from Dave's Bait and Tackle."

"Oh yeah, I know Dave," Skimpy Bathing Suit said. "Good guy."

"So, Dave was able to bring your boat in? What kind is it?"

"It's just a fishing boat," Stan said. "It's not much, but it does the job. Dave didn't have any trouble towing it back."

"Then what?" I asked.

"Well, there was no sign of Nevin," Stan said. "Like I said, the boat was empty. So, I decided to take it back out and search for him myself. I knew he had his life preserver, so I thought I might find him floating. Or, I thought he maybe could have ended up on shore, in one of those remote areas that would have made it difficult for him to find his way back into town. So, I got into the boat and was going around the lake, and that's when I saw it." His eyes went wide, and he started coughing again.

"Saw what?" Skimpy Bathing Suit asked, his eyes mirroring Stan's.

"The water nymph!" gasped one of the members of the crowd. She was very young, with a head of flaming red hair and a red and yellow bikini. "You saw the water nymph, didn't you?"

"They're NOT water nymphs," Stan sputtered through his coughs. "The correct term is 'naiads.'"

"Oh, sorry ... I didn't realize the water nymph had a name," Red Hair said. "Naiad, the water nymph."

Stan's face turned purple as he struggled to explain the terminology, and I put my hand on his arm. "Stan, what did you see? Was it the naiad?"

He sucked in another deep breath and shook his head. "No. I saw the plesiosaur."

Red Hair gave a little shriek. "We have another monster in the lake? How many monsters are actually in there?"

"He's talking about Locky," Pat said. "Many scientists and experts think the Loch Ness Monster is actually a plesiosaur."

"Oh," Red Hair said, sounding relieved.

The rescuer was staring at Stan. "You saw Locky?" His voice was hushed and full of reverence. "You are so lucky. I have been coming to this lake for years trying to get a glimpse of him."

"No, you don't understand," Stan said. "Locky ate Nevin."

There was a short silence before Red Hair spoke again.

"No, that's not right," she said, her voice confident. "Locky wouldn't eat anyone. You just said he's a plesiosaur. They only eat plants."

"That's a brontosaur," Stan said. "Plesiosaurs are carnivores."

"Well, that doesn't mean he would eat a human," Red Hair said. She looked around the crowd. "Right?"

"Locky has never eaten anyone before," Skimpy Bathing Suit added.

"Not that we know of," another member of the crowd, an older man wearing a bright-green bathing suit and unbuttoned green plaid shirt that exposed a significant paunch, said darkly.

"That's true," Stan said. "But you also have a long history of bodies not resurfacing in this lake. Sure, it's possible it's because of how cold and deep it is, but what if it's because something is actually eating them?"

"Ugh, gross," Red Hair said.

"Hold on," I said. "Can we back up here? Do you have a reason to think Locky ate Nevin, as opposed to something else happening to him? I mean, are we even sure Nevin is dead?"

"He must be," Stan insisted. "I found the boat, but not him."

"But as you pointed out, he could still be floating somewhere, or washed up on shore somewhere else," I reminded him. "We don't know for sure what happened to him."

But Stan was vigorously shaking his head. "I'm sure he's gone. The plesiosaur ate him."

"I can't believe Locky would do that," Skimpy Bathing Suit said.

"I can," Green Bathing Suit countered. "He's a monster. That's what monsters do."

I held up my hand. "Why don't you tell us why you think Nevin was, err, eaten?"

"I already did," Stan answered, his voice rising in agitation. "I saw the plesiosaur."

"Okay, okay," I said, keeping my voice soothing. "You saw the plesiosaur. Where were you when you saw it?"

"I was in the boat," Stan said. "I was rowing. Or trying to row. I couldn't get the motor started."

"Couldn't Dave have helped you?" Skimpy Bathing Suit asked.

Stan grimaced. "I'd already sent him away. Told him I was fine. So, I tried and tried, but it just wouldn't start. I was using the oars instead, but it was really difficult. I was having trouble steering, and I felt like I was just going around in circles. I finally just stopped. I needed a break, so I started scanning the lake. I was trying to see if I could spot Nevin somewhere, you know, maybe bobbing along in his life jacket. But then ..." He paused dramatically, and the entire crowd took a step closer to him.

"But then?" Skimpy Bathing Suit asked.

"But then, I saw it. The head and neck rose out of the lake. It was like a hundred feet away from me."

"A hundred feet!" Skimpy Bathing Suit couldn't believe it. "Man, some people have all the luck."

"It was NOT lucky," Stan said. "It was horrible and terrifying. I was so startled, I fell off the bench and onto the floor of the boat. His head ..." Stan squeezed his eyes shut tightly, his Adam's apple bobbing as he swallowed.

"His head what?" Skimpy Bathing Suit prompted.

"His head ... swung over toward me, and he stared at me. Right into my eyes. And that's when I knew! He knew I was Nevin's friend. And he was letting me know he ate him!"

"Um ..." There were so many questions running through my head, I had no idea where to even start. How does a plesiosaur look when it's communicating that it ate someone? And how would it possibly know Nevin was his friend? Moreover, why would it care?

Stan didn't seem to notice my puzzlement, because he continued ploughing on with his story. "I'll never forget the look in his eyes. It was so cold! I was sure I was goner ... that he was going to eat me just like he ate Nevin."

"So, what happened?" Skimpy Bathing Suit asked, taking another step closer, his eyes bright.

"I fell out of the boat!" Stan exclaimed.

"Wait, you fell out of the boat, and Locky didn't try to eat you?" Green Bathing Suit asked.

Stan pressed his fingers against his temples as he shook his head. "I'm so confused! I don't know what happened. I was trying to get away. I picked up the oars, but they fell out of their little holes, and then I hit myself on the head ..."

"You hit yourself on the head with an oar?" Green Bathing Suit asked, his voice dripping with skepticism. "How did you manage that?"

"Oh, I don't know. I was trying to get the oar back into the little hole, but I was sure the plesiosaur was coming ... I could *feel* him coming, and I was trying to hurry and ... I just don't know. It's all so confusing."

There was a long silence. "So, you fell out of the boat trying to get away from Locky," I said. "And the reason Locky was coming toward you was because he wanted to eat you, just as he'd eaten Nevin?"

Stan shook his head "yes." "I thought I was going to die," he said, and again, he started coughing. His face was turning an unhealthy shade of purple, and I began to worry he might be experiencing some bad effects of being in the lake.

"Why don't we get you to the hospital? Then, we can deal with Nevin," I said.

"I don't need to go to the hospital," Stan uttered between coughs. "I'm fine. And there's nothing to deal with, when it comes to Nevin. He's gone."

"Yes, but don't you think you should file a missing person's report?"

"Why?" Stan asked, a bewildered expression on his face. "Nevin isn't missing. I told you where he is. That plesiosaur ate him and then almost ate me."

Inwardly, I sighed. "Okay, but the police still need to look for him. There still needs to be a paper trail. You're doing this research together, right? Well, I'm guessing that whoever you work for is going to want something more official than just your word that Nevin was eaten by an ancient dinosaur."

Stan frowned. "Oh, I forgot about that. Yes, paperwork. Everything needs to be buttoned up. I's dotted and T's crossed." He sighed.

"Yes, so let's get you to the hospital, and then to the police station," I said, holding my hand out. He stared at me for a moment longer, as if debating how trustworthy I was before allowing me to help him to his feet. He was heavier than he looked, and I probably wouldn't have been able to do it alone. Luckily, though, Skimpy Bathing Suit swooped in to give me a hand.

"I just can't believe Locky would eat anyone," Skimpy Bathing Suit said again, incredulously.

Chapter 3

"So, what do you think?" I asked Officer Brandon Wyle. We were standing in the hallway outside of Stan's hospital room. Wyle had started by questioning Stan, and then, he took my statement.

"I think it's uncanny, how you always happen to be in the middle of these things," Wyle said. As soon as he had seen me in the hospital, he rolled his eyes and muttered "Of course."

Wyle and I had a bit of a history. I liked to think of us as partners in solving cases, whereas he would prefer I solely focused on growing the herbs and flowers I put in my teas and tinctures. He was a big believer that professionals should be the ones focused on solving crime, not regular civilians. Especially regular civilians who sold tea out of their homes.

But it wasn't my fault that my clients kept running into trouble with the law. And it also wasn't my fault that I had a knack for solving cases.

"I actually agree—it's uncanny," I said. "But that's not what I was asking. Do you think it's possible that Nevin is still alive out there somewhere?"

"It's possible," Wyle said. "I've already called it in, and I've got people searching the lake. But it depends on how long he's been out there. Even though it's June, the water is still pretty cold. If he didn't drown, it's possible he could die of exposure."

"In the summer?"

Wyle shrugged. "Like I said, the lake is cold. And if he was out there all night, it's a possibility."

"So, does that mean it's true about bodies? That they aren't found?"

"Pretty much." Wyle tucked his notebook back in his pocket. "I know it's fashionable to think we don't recover bodies because it's Redemption, but there's an actual scientific reason behind it. Cold, deep lakes like this one don't give up their dead."

I shivered. I could almost feel icy, dead fingers trailing down my spine.

He noticed, and his dark eyes sharpened. He was a good-looking guy, with high cheekbones, a square jaw, and dark hair that always seemed too long, like he was in constant need of a haircut. "It's perfectly safe, if you swim in the designated areas by the beaches," he said.

"So, it's not safe if you swim somewhere else?" I asked while folding my arms across my chest, suddenly conscious of my bathing suit underneath the white tunic coverup.

"It's definitely more of a risk," he said. "People have drowned swimming in the middle of the lake. Good swimmers, too. They were out in a boat with friends and decided to jump in and … well …" Wyle shook his head. "It doesn't help, not being able to recover the bodies. They just disappear in the water. Never come back up. That's probably why these stories of Locky and the water nymph are so prevalent. It's easier to believe they were grabbed by something and dragged away or eaten, rather than getting caught up in some sort of deadly undertow."

"They're called 'naiads,' not 'water nymphs,'" I corrected.

"Oh, that's right. Stan already admonished me." Wyle shook his head. "Anyway, whatever it's called, I doubt it had anything to do with Nevin's disappearance."

"What do you think happened to him?"

"I have no idea," Wyle said. "That's why it's called 'investigating.'"

I rolled my eyes. "Ha. Are there any obvious signs? Like blood in the bottom of the boat, or his briefcase washed up on shore?"

"Right now, no. We just found the boat. It was floating in the middle of the lake, and we're checking that for evidence. We're also searching the lake, but nothing has turned up yet."

"Any sign of Locky?"

Wyle's lips quirked up. "None, I'm afraid."

I chewed on my lip. "Does this happen a lot? People coming in saying they saw Locky?"

"Enough," Wyle said. "Although I have to say Stan's account is more ... colorful, than we normally get. Usually, the stories are from people standing on the shoreline, convinced they saw something across the lake. It's not uncommon for there to be alcohol involved. Occasionally, we get pictures, but so far, they've all been debunked as something else ... like a floating log or a swimming deer. But Locky attacking someone in a boat? That's a first."

"Was Stan drinking? Or maybe on drugs?"

"We won't know for sure until the tests come back, but the doctor doesn't think so. He's not acting impaired in any way."

"Other than thinking a plesiosaur was trying to eat him," I said.

Wyle's lips quirked up again. "Yeah, other than that. It's also possible this is some sort of side effect from his concussion."

"Concussion? So he did hit his head with an oar?"

"I don't know if it was an oar or not, but yes, he has a nasty bump on the head and a mild concussion. And hallucinations are definitely possible after a brain injury."

"So, Locky was a hallucination?"

"That would be my guess."

That made the most sense. Stan hadn't seemed impaired to me, either. "So, if Nevin did drown, you don't think we're going to find his body," I assumed.

"If history is any indication, unfortunately, probably not. We're combing the area and trying to find witnesses to see if anyone saw Nevin in his boat. And we're talking to Dave, of course. But I don't know." Wyle's expression cracked, and I could see the hopelessness leaking out. "It's not looking good. If there's no evidence of foul play, I'm not sure what we can do. It's not against the law for an adult to disappear."

"Wait ... you think Nevin staged this?"

Wyle shrugged. "It's possible. If you wanted to fake your own death via drowning so you could start somewhere else, Angel's Lake would be the one to do it in. No one is going to find it odd that the body never surfaces. All he needs to do is untie the boat, push it out to the lake, and walk away. Poof. Everyone assumes he drowned, or in this case, was eaten by a prehistoric dinosaur, and he's free and clear."

I frowned. What Wyle said made a lot of sense—Nevin faked his drowning so he could disappear—but I was having trouble believing it. When I pictured his excitement in Nancy's lobby, how he couldn't wait to investigate the lake, it was hard to believe he would simply walk away from his work. Nevin hadn't struck me as much of an actor.

Wyle was watching my face closely. "You aren't buying it."

"Well ... it makes sense," I said. "It's a sound theory. And Nevin did know about the lake's history and how rarely bodies surface. But ..."

Wyle raised an eyebrow. "But ..."

"You didn't see his passion for what he was doing. He couldn't wait to publish his research and set the scientific community on fire. If he fakes his death, all of that goes away. Now, granted, I barely met him, but from what I saw, I just don't buy it."

"Hmm. How did Nevin and Stan get along?"

"Fine. At least, from the little I could tell." I thought about the interaction we'd had at the Redemption Inn. "They seemed to have similar personalities and communication styles. It made sense that they were partners."

"No tension or fighting?"

"Not that I could tell. Nancy might know more. I just saw them for a few minutes. I mean, they had that sort of sibling energy, where they might squabble sometimes, but they were also best of friends. Speaking of siblings ... does Nevin have any family?"

"A sister," Wyle said. "I'm going to reach out to her. According to Stan, all Nevin's clothes and personal belongings are still here, so I'm going to see if his sister will come pick them up."

"Speaking of belongings, I wonder what's going to happen with the research if Nevin doesn't turn up," I said.

"I don't know, but that's definitely on our list to find out," Wyle said.

Chapter 4

"So, Wyle thinks Nevin faked his death," Pat said. We were back in my kitchen, cups of tea in front of us. The setting sun slanted through the windows, turning the light a warm, orangey red.

While Pat dropped Daphne off at home, I had left Stan at the Redemption Inn. The doctors thought his concussion was mild enough to not require observation, but they wanted him to stay put in the hotel for a few days. Stan didn't have any objections as, according to him, he still had research to finish up.

"You need to rest," the doctor said, eyeing him over his glasses.

"I will," Stan said. "Once my research is done."

"Are you going to make me admit you?" the doctor asked.

After a lot of talk, Stan finally capitulated, promising to at least take it easy.

"Yeah, but I don't buy it," I said. "Nevin was way too excited about this research and what it would mean once he published it. I can't see him abandoning it."

"Maybe he didn't have a choice," Pat said. "Maybe there was something else going on ... like he was being blackmailed, or something."

I raised an eyebrow. "Blackmailed?"

"Yeah, you know. Maybe he owed someone money." Pat's face lit up as she indulged the theory. "Maybe he gambled and borrowed money from the wrong people."

"Nevin didn't strike me as someone who was trying to run away from loan sharks," I said. "And if he was, I suspect they would want something a little more convincing than him maybe drowning in a cold lake. Like, a body."

"Well, maybe it wasn't loan sharks, then," Pat said. "Maybe it was something else."

"What, like the scientific community?" I asked, my tone disbelieving. "This so-called evidence was so earth-shattering that someone decided to blackmail him, and whatever they had on him was so bad, he thought it would be better to fake his own death?"

"Why not?" Pat argued. "You said how thorough they wanted to be … have all their I's dotted and T's crossed."

"They were certainly concerned about that," I said thoughtfully. "Although, it's just as possible that their research isn't as groundbreaking as they think."

"That doesn't mean the scientific community would know that," Pat said. "It's possible someone out there is very worried about what they're going to release, or what they think they're going to release."

"Yes, but Stan is still around," I said. "Surely, he can publish the paper without Nevin."

"Unless Nevin disappeared *with* the research," Pat theorized.

"Yeah, it's not clear what Nevin had or didn't have," I said. "Stan was going to go through Nevin's things to pack them up for his sister. He also didn't give us a straight answer about what was going to happen with the research. He just kept talking about all the work he had to do to sort things out."

"Would be interesting to know," Pat said.

"I can ask when I drop by," I offered.

Pat gave me a look. "You're dropping by?"

I rolled my eyes. "Oh, please. The doctor wanted someone to check on Stan, and I volunteered. There didn't seem to be anyone else, and I don't mind. I have to drop off tea orders anyway tomorrow, so it's on my route."

"Well, definitely see if you can find out more about this research," Pat said.

"Yeah, that does feel like it might be the key," I said.

Chapter 5

"Charlie, you're back," Nancy called out from behind the front desk as I stepped into the Redemption Inn, her face wreathed in a smile. "Twice in one week. I can't believe it. I must be blessed."

"You're definitely blessed," I said as I made my way toward her, breathing in the scents of lemon furniture polish and freshly brewed coffee. "Although it doesn't hurt that you've got a local celebrity staying here."

Nancy's smiled turned wry. "Ah, yes. And he's a bit of a handful, just as you would imagine a celebrity would be."

"That must be fun."

She shook her head. "Oh yeah. Tons."

There was paperwork spread out in front of Nancy, and her silver glasses were once again perched on her nose. I leaned forward, careful not to disturb her piles. "So, I guess he's not resting like he's supposed to."

"Ah, no. He's, well, I'm not sure what he's doing." She sighed. "At least he's upstairs and not down here."

"Was he down here a lot before?"

"Not since Nevin disappeared ... or was eaten, or whatever." She removed her glasses and pinched the bridge of her nose. "But before that, if they weren't at the lake, I couldn't get rid of them."

"What, they just hung out here in the lobby?"

"No, in the breakfast area." She waved to the room off to the side, which was filled with tables and chairs. "Normally, I don't care if my guests want to sit in there and enjoy a cup of coffee and cookie. You know how I always have the coffee pot on. But those two were constantly asking for something."

"Like what?"

She started ticking off her fingers. "More coffee. More hot water. Cold water. Another tea bag. More lemons. More cream.

A pen. A pencil. A pencil sharpener. An eraser. A stapler. A paperclip. Tape. Batteries."

"Batteries?"

She nodded. "Yeah, it was crazy. I don't know how they got any investigating done at all, as all they seemed to be doing was asking for things. And bickering."

My eyes narrowed. "Bickering?"

She made a face. "It was like listening to an old married couple. It wasn't like they were fighting per se, just bickering."

"Like they were brothers."

Nancy's eyes lit up. "Oooh, yes. Brothers. That's probably a better comparison."

"Was there anything else odd or different that you noticed?"

"You mean more than I already mentioned?" Nancy frowned. "No, that was pretty much it."

"I suppose that also means you didn't see anything the night Nevin disappeared?"

"No, I didn't. I didn't even realize he had gone out."

The sound of a door slamming upstairs floated down. Nancy sighed.

"Stan?" I asked.

"Who else?" She sighed again. "Maybe you can settle him down a bit. This can't be good for his concussion."

"I'll do my best," I said as I headed up the stairs.

I found Stan not in his room, but in the one next door. He was muttering to himself as he sat on the floor, pawing through a stack of clothes. The room was a disaster, with papers strewn everywhere and suitcases lying open on their side. Even the sheets were stripped from the bed.

"Stan?" I asked, my voice hesitant as I cautiously made my way into the room. "What are you doing?"

"What does it look like?" he returned, tossing a shirt over his shoulder.

"It looks like you aren't resting the way you're supposed to," I said.

"I'm fine," he said.

He didn't look fine, but I wasn't sure if telling him so would make things worse or better. "Is this Nevin's room?"

"Who else's would it be?"

"Are you going to answer all my questions with a question?" I asked.

That got him to pause. He looked up, squinting at me from behind his glasses. "That depends," he said.

"On what?"

"On the type of questions you ask me."

"What's the right type?"

"Not the dumb kind." He went back to digging through the pile of clothes.

Things weren't going very well. I watched him for a few minutes. His skin was waxy, and there were deep purple bruises under his eyes. "Okay, so what about this? You tell me what you're doing, or I call 9-1-1 and have them take you back to the hospital."

His head snapped up. "You wouldn't."

"Oh, but I would," I said.

He stared at me, furrowing his brow in confusion. "But why? You don't even know me. Why do you care?"

I knelt down in front of him. "Stan, you look like crap," I said. "You need to rest, and you aren't. I know I don't know you, but that doesn't mean I want to watch something bad happen to you, and right now, it looks like that's exactly what is going to happen."

He was silent for a moment, thinking about what I said. "I'm looking for some important notes."

I glanced around at the disaster surrounding us. "I take it Nevin had them last."

"I thought I did," he fussed. "But I can't find them in either room."

"Are you sure Nevin didn't take them with him?"

Stan shook his head. "No! We never took our files or notes with us on the boat. We brought a notebook, of course, so we could take notes, but never anything else. We would never risk getting them wet or losing them."

"Do you think Nevin put them somewhere else?" I asked.

"I don't know why he would do that," Stan said. "We kept all our files together in one place."

"And you're sure they're not there?"

He rubbed his forehead. "I've checked, doubled-checked, and triple-checked. They're not there, and I can't find them."

His voice was getting more and more agitated, and I started to get concerned about his health. I crouched down next to him. "I think we should take a break."

He stared at me in alarm. "I can't take a break! I have too much to do."

"You can, and you will," I said firmly. "Sifting through a pile of clothes for the umpteenth time isn't going to find those files. But maybe if you take a break and we talk about it, you might think of a new direction or place to look. Not to mention you really look like you could use a break."

Stan looked away. It was clear he was torn—on one hand, he didn't want to stop looking, but on the other, he knew what I said made a lot of sense.

"Fine," he said, a little ungraciously. "Where did you want to take this break?"

I almost said, "Aunt May's Diner," as I was sure Nancy didn't want to see him sitting in her breakfast room outside of breakfast anymore, but another look at his sickly expression made me realize I couldn't justify taking him out. He should be close to his room, so he could lie down if need be. "Let's just go downstairs and have a cup a coffee or tea," I suggested.

Stan's expression softened. "Nancy does have good coffee."

"Then it's settled." I helped him up, crossing my fingers that Nancy wouldn't strangle me. Maybe her next tea order should be on the house.

"If we're lucky, she might even have some fresh-baked cookies," I said as I guided him out of the room. "She's famous for her ginger snaps."

"I shouldn't be eating cookies," he said as he licked his lips.

"Yeah, I shouldn't either, but I usually make an exception for Nancy's," I said.

We entered the lobby just as Nancy was placing a plate of cookies in front of a young couple sitting on the overstuffed couch. She straightened, her expression hopeful. "Are you two going out somewhere?"

"Actually, I thought maybe you wouldn't mind if we sat in there," I gestured with my head, trying to communicate with my eyes how I truly wouldn't be doing this to her if I had another choice.

Nancy's eyes narrowed, but she kept her voice pleasant. "Of course," she said. "I suppose you'd like a cup of coffee?"

"If it's not too much trouble," I said.

"A cookie, too, would be nice," Stan added.

It was all I could do not to kick him. Nancy's smile turned frosty. "Of course."

"I can help," I quickly offered.

"No, no, no," she said, flapping her hand. "I'm happy to do it. Go make yourself comfortable, and I'll bring them out."

Stan was already heading over to the breakfast room. I glanced back at Nancy and mouthed "sorry." She shrugged and gave me a lopsided smile. "It's fine," she mouthed back. "Part of the job."

I supposed she had a point. I turned to follow Stan into the breakfast area.

He had already chosen a table, one near the window, and was making himself comfortable. There were probably a dozen tables with accompanying chairs scattered around the center of the room. A long countertop stretched across two of the walls. It was empty, other than a couple of baskets of flowers, but in the morning, it would be filled with a large selection of breakfast items.

I had just gotten myself seated when Nancy appeared again, holding a tray loaded with two mugs and a plate of cookies. She placed the coffee in front of Stan and gave me a mug of hot water and a tea infuser filled with my own brand.

"Oh, you didn't have to do that," I said, touched. Nancy knew I wasn't a big fan of coffee. I did drink it on occasion, usually when I hadn't gotten a decent night's sleep and needed the caffeine, but I certainly wasn't going to ask for tea now.

"Of course I did," she said, winking. "I know much you love your tea."

I smiled and picked up the tea infuser to place in the mug. Stan took a big gulp of coffee and reached for a cookie.

"Okay, so let's talk about these notes," I said. "When was the last time you saw them?"

He huffed an exasperated sigh. "That's part of the problem. I can't really remember."

"Well, when *do* you remember seeing them?"

He thought. "Two days ago. In the morning."

"So, the day Nevin disappeared?"

Stan gave me a look. "He didn't disappear. He was eaten."

"But it was that day, right?"

"Yes." He took a bite of the cookie. "We were going through the notes after breakfast, before we went out for the day."

"When you decided to go out for the day, what did you do with your notes?"

"Well, we would have packed them away in our traveling briefcase. It opens like an accordion, and we put all the files there."

"And you keep that in one of your rooms?"

"Yes."

"Which one?"

"It depends. It generally just went with whoever was putting it away."

"Okay, so which room was it in that day?"

"Nevin's. No," he squished up his face. "Mine."

"And you haven't looked for it again until now?"

"No, we did," Stan said. "When we were done at the lake, we updated the files with our notes. I remember doing that after dinner. I just can't remember if those specific pages were in there. But they must have been." Stan started to push back his chair. "Oh, this isn't helping. I just need to keep searching."

"Hang on," I said, placing my hand on his arm. "Maybe we talk about something else and see if it jogs your memory?"

He eyed me suspiciously. "What do you want to talk about?"

"Well, it's just ..." I paused and picked up my tea, trying to figure out the best way to ask my question without causing him to storm back upstairs. The more I listened to Stan go on about the missing notes, the more convinced I was that Nevin had faked his own death and run off with them. "I know the cops haven't finished their investigation yet, but as of now, they haven't found any evidence of Nevin at the lake." This wasn't exactly true, as I hadn't spoken to Wyle that day, but I felt like I needed a way to ease into the questions I wanted to ask.

"That's not surprising," Stan said, picking up his coffee mug and taking another loud slurp. "Even if Nevin hadn't been eaten, the lake is so cold and deep, his body wouldn't be found."

"That's true," I said. "But there is another possible explanation."

"What?"

"That he was never on the lake in the first place."

Stan stared at me, his expression confused. "Of course he went out on the lake. Where else would he have gone?"

"Well, that's the thing. Maybe something else happened to him."

"Like what?"

"Like any number of things. Something could have happened to him on the way to the lake. Or, maybe he faked his own death."

Stan blinked. "What? Nevin wouldn't do that."

"How do you know? You're the one who keeps talking about how big this scientific finding you've discovered is ... how it's going to rock the scientific community. Maybe he got cold feet or was threatened."

Stan's eyes widened. "Threatened?"

"I don't know. I'm just throwing things out. But you did say you didn't actually see him go out on the lake. No one else seems to have seen him out there, either. So ..." I held out my hands. "Can we be so sure he ever did?"

Stan looked flustered. "He said he was going on the lake. He wouldn't lie to me."

"He would if he wanted to protect you," I said gently.

"Protect me from what?"

"The reason he faked his own death, if that's what he did," I said.

"You really think Nevin was being threatened?"

"Again, I don't know. What do *you* think? Do you think there could be someone in the scientific community who would have threatened Nevin to keep your work from being published?"

"I ... I don't know." He sounded bewildered. "Maybe. Nevin did have more connections to the community than I did. I guess it's possible someone reached out to him, and Nevin never told me."

"Where do you two work?"

Stan shifted uncomfortably. "That's complicated."

"What do you mean?"

"We're kind of ... between opportunities."

I did a double take. "You're *what?*"

"Well, this work is so important," Stan said. "We need to focus our full attention on it. Once it's published, there will be no end to the opportunities."

I gave him a look. "In other words, you're unemployed."

He ducked his head. "You make it sound worse than it is."

"I'm not trying to make it sound good or bad. I'm just trying to understand. May I ask how you ended up without employment?"

He sighed. "Nevin was trying to get a new cryptozoology program started."

"'Cryptozoology'?"

He eyed me. "It's the study of unknown animals, referred to as 'cryptids,' and it involves the application of science in the pursuit of finding new species and hybrid animals. It's a perfectly legitimate form of scientific exploration."

"He's a professor?"

"We're both professors. I was in the paleontology department when we met. Nevin had this brilliant idea to form a new field of study that combined cryptozoology with paranormal research to specifically focus on so-called 'supernatural' or 'mythical' beings. While there are universities and colleges that have cryptozoology and paranormal departments, none of them combine the two to focus specifically on these types of beings. Nevin even had a name for it: para-cryptozoology. He was sure this new department and major would be a huge draw for students, but unfortunately, the faculty members and dean didn't recognize his genius."

"They didn't start the new program," I said.

"They wouldn't even give us the courtesy of forming a committee to talk about it," Stan said mournfully. "It was incredibly disrespectful. Nevin was furious."

"So, you both quit?"

Stan nodded. "I had always been intrigued with the field of cryptozoology, and even though my background wasn't an exact fit, I started helping him out. I had planned to transfer to the new department as soon as it was up and running. Of course, that didn't happen."

All the pieces were starting to come together. "This research was supposed to help get this new field of study started," I said.

"Exactly. We were going to show the world that combining cryptozoology and paranormal was the next level of scientific study. Not to mention how necessary the research is, in and of itself." He flapped his hands, nearly knocking over his coffee cup. "Can you imagine how many beings there are out there that we don't know about? They know about US, of course, and because humans are so woefully ignorant of their very existence, they're able to get away with all sorts of mischief. But if we can start to pull the curtain back and prove they truly exist—that they're not just make-believe or stories or myths—then everything changes. We can start to fight back."

I leaned back slightly from the table. "'Fight back'?"

"Yes, fight back." Stan pounded his fist on the table, disrupting the coffee cup, a strange gleam in his eye. "Do you have any idea how many unexplained events happen each year? And so many of them are dangerous to humans. All the single car crashes on lonely stretches of road. No sign of mechanical failure, no alcohol or drugs in the driver's system, no sign of heart attack or anything like that. No detectible reason for the car to crash, and yet it did. Or what about all the people who have gone missing in the national parks each year? No one knows what happened to them. They simply vanish without a trace."

"And you think these things are all because of … supernatural beings?" I asked.

"Well, do you have a better explanation?" Stan demanded.

"I … I'm not sure," I said.

"There are so many beings out there we have not adequately studied," he continued. "Take ghosts, for instance. Despite *so many* confirmed sightings of ghosts out there, many people don't believe. And because of that, they sometimes put themselves in great danger. And that barely scratches the surface of mystical creatures. The faery kingdom alone is so large and complex, it should have its own field of study." He paused to pick up his mug and realized it was empty. "It's absurd, how we don't take this more seriously. Do you see Nancy?" He craned his neck as he looked around.

"You and Nevin were in agreement on this?" I asked, deliberately ignoring his Nancy question.

He turned back to me, furrowing his brows. "Of course. Why would you ask?"

"No big reason. You calling for Nancy just made me think of it." I took a sip of tea.

That got his attention. He put his cup down. "What does that mean?"

"It's just …" I shrugged and laughed a little. "Nancy heard you two arguing, is all."

"What?" His eyes widened. "No, we weren't arguing. We never argue."

"Bickering, maybe."

"No, we don't bicker, either," he said, but there was a slight hesitation.

"Well, I guess she misinterpreted what she heard."

"I mean, it's true we have some … professional disagreements," Nevin acquiesced. "But that's to be expected."

Aha. I carefully put my cup down. "Were you having professional disagreements here?"

"Yes, but they were nothing! We just … well, truly it's nothing. Just a difference of opinion as to what we should do with the research."

"I thought you both wanted to publish it."

"We do! Errr, did. Well, I still plan to publish it as soon as I can, once this has all passed. To honor Nevin's legacy."

"Of course," I said. "But what was the disagreement about, then?"

"It's … well, Nevin thought it would be smart to go back to our old university with it first. He thought if they saw what we had discovered, they'd not only rehire us, but we'd be able to start the new department. Plus, getting published would be easier if we were affiliated with a university."

"That sounds like a good plan. You disagreed?"

"It was a ridiculous plan," Stan said disgustedly. "They wouldn't take us seriously until we had the research in black and white. I don't even understand why he'd want to give them that option. The whole experience was humiliating. Besides, I think Nevin was thinking too small. Once the scientific community sees what we've discovered, we'd have our pick of offers."

"Stan, there you are." Wyle appeared at the entrance of the breakfast room. He glanced at me, and I could almost see him sigh. "I have some news."

"What?" Stan asked, struggling to his feet, but Wyle waved him back down as he strode across the room.

"Stay where you are. It's better if you're sitting."

Stan's eyes widened, and his face turned a shade paler. "Why?"

Wyle waited until he was standing in front of Nevin. "I'm so sorry to have to tell you this, but we found a body that may be Nevin's."

Stan blinked rapidly from behind his glasses. "You … you found Nevin?"

Wyle nodded. "At least, that's how it appears. We need you to come to the station to identify him."

"But … but Nevin was eaten," Stan insisted yet again.

Wyle glanced at me, his face grim, and nodded. "The body we found has bite marks on it."

Chapter 6

"So, Locky really did eat Nevin?" I asked Wyle in a low, incredulous voice. We were standing in the hallway at the police station. Stan had just finished identifying Nevin and was in the bathroom. His skin definitely had a greenish tone to it. I hoped he wasn't sick in there.

"'Eaten' is kind of a strong word," Wyle said. "There were bite marks on the body, but it was intact. More like Locky just gnawed on him for a bit."

I made a face. "Ugh. That's an image I don't want in my head."

Wyle half-smiled. "I don't think it was Locky. Putting aside the question of whether or not Locky even exists, the bite marks are peculiar."

"How so?"

"Well, if Locky is a carnivore, then why didn't he actually eat Nevin? Why just bite him?"

"Maybe it wasn't Locky?"

"Same question. Why just bite? Besides, there's nothing in that lake that matches the jaw and teeth marks. At least, that's what the ME thinks. He's going to send it to another lab and make some calls."

"Speaking of the lake, I thought if Nevin had drowned, his body would never surface."

"Yeah, that's what normally happens. I don't know why his body turned up. That's another question for the ME."

"Where did you find him?"

"He was tangled up in the weeds near the shore, a ways up from the beach. It was a pretty remote area. We were lucky to find him."

"How *did* you find him?"

"One of our deputies happened to see a flash of something in the weeds, like light reflecting off of a piece of jewelry or watch. He went to check it out, although ..." Wyle frowned.

"There was no watch or jewelry on the body. So, I don't know what he saw, but whatever it was, it was a good thing he did."

"That's pretty remarkable, all things considered," I said.

"Yeah, I agree. It doesn't happen a lot, but sometimes, things go our way. And I'm always grateful when they do." He glanced at the door to the men's room. "I probably should go check on Stan."

"I'm wondering if he should be back in the hospital," I said. "He didn't look good before, and with this latest shock, it might be too much for him."

Wyle pushed open the door and poked his head in. "Stan? You okay?"

There was a strangled moan. Wyle made a face as he stepped into the men's room.

I stayed where I was, figuring Stan might need me once Wyle delivered him from the bathroom. But the longer I stayed, the more I realized there seemed to be a lot of commotion from the front of the station where the dispatch was.

I headed down the hallway toward the noise. I couldn't really figure out what was going on—all I could hear was a lot of upset talking in loud voices.

When I finally reached the front, though, I could see why. It was pandemonium. The phones were ringing off the hook, and there was a line of civilians waiting to talk to deputies.

I noticed a female deputy standing by the water cooler, getting a drink. Her face was flushed, and her hair was falling out of its bun. She looked like she was just trying to take a break from the chaos. I edged closer to her.

"What's going on?" I asked.

She eyed me. "Locky. All these people are either claiming to have seen Locky, or are afraid of seeing him. They're all worried he's going to start devouring people."

I closed my eyes briefly. Clearly, word had gotten out about Nevin.

Someone called the deputy's name, and she glanced behind her. "I have to go."

"I was afraid of this," Wyle said in my ear. I jumped, startled on a number of levels.

He noticed and flashed a sideways smile. "Sorry."

"I thought you were with Stan?"

"I was. He needs a few more minutes, and then it would probably be good to take him back to the hotel. Preferably through the back."

I nodded before turning back to the crazy scene in front of us. "How do you think they found out about Nevin?"

"It's a small town. How do you think?" Wyle sighed and pinched the bridge of his nose. "All I know is it's going to be a late night. All hands on deck, patrolling the lake and chasing after a made-up monster. I'm going to need more coffee."

"At the very least, get your coffee from somewhere else," I said. "Don't drink the sludge in there." I gestured toward the break room.

He flashed one of his crooked grins, which was always dangerous. "Are you offering?"

"I'll have a fresh pot ready. And I might even throw in a few cookies," I said, easing back a step. Always good to put some space between Wyle and me, I figured, especially after a grin like that. "But remember our deal." I wagged my finger at his chest.

"I remember. Information for food."

"Exactly," I said cheerfully.

Chapter 7

"I can't believe it. Locky really did eat Nevin!" Pat proclaimed. We were in my kitchen, cups of tea and my famous chocolate chip cookies in front of us. Midnight was curled up in the sun on his usual chair. I had just finished filling Pat in on my conversations with Nancy and Stan at the Redemption Inn, and of course, about finding Nevin's body.

"Well, if he was trying to, he did a pretty bad job of it," I said.

"There were bite marks."

"Exactly. Bite *marks*. Not actual bites," I said, picking up my tea as Pat reached for a cookie. "What self-respecting Loch Ness Monster doesn't finish its food?"

Pat eyed me. "How many Loch Ness Monsters do you know?"

"I know he wouldn't last very long without actual food."

"Maybe he was playing with his meal, like a cat," Pat said.

Midnight opened an eye and looked at her.

"Maybe there wasn't a monster at all," I said.

"Then what did the teeth marks come from?"

"That is the question of the hour," I said. "My guess is, it was some other animal, like a bear. Or maybe a mountain lion."

"So, the mountain lion was playing with its food?"

Midnight raised his head and gave us both a dirty look, flicking his tail in disgust.

"That makes more sense than a make-believe monster doing so," I said.

"Okay, but I've never heard of a mountain lion doing that," Pat said.

"That's the point," I explained. "Predators don't usually play with their food. They usually eat what they kill, unless it's a mom protecting her baby, but she'll usually tear a threat apart, as well. If there truly was some sort of Loch Ness Monster, I don't know why it would just give Nevin a few love bites and call it a day."

"It is perplexing," Pat agreed. "But it's not the only perplexing part of this case. I'm still trying to wrap my head around the fact that Stan and Nevin aren't employed."

"It's hard to believe," I said.

"It's also hard to believe they didn't think through quitting their teaching jobs," Pat mused. "They were probably tenured. And they left because of what? Hurt feelings? And without any plan as to getting hired somewhere else?"

"Yeah, you'd think they would have done something ... maybe take a sabbatical. Or if they couldn't do that, maybe wait for the yearly school breaks, and do their research then," I said. "Why quit first? Why not wait until they have something, and then try and use that to negotiate or find something else?"

"The whole thing is strange," Pat said. "Do you think Nevin got cold feet?"

"Possibly," I said. "It doesn't make sense, why he would go out in the boat by himself at night ... unless maybe he was feeling desperate. He wanted something that would make a strong case, so he could get his job back."

"Makes sense," Pat said. "Nevin was worried, but Stan wasn't, so Stan didn't feel the need to go out in the boat at night."

"Neither one of them look particularly athletic, either," I added. "So my guess is that Nevin wasn't a whole lot better with the boat than Stan was. It's not all that surprising that he didn't make it back in one piece."

"Ah, so maybe what happened is, Nevin ticked off Locky," Pat said. "Maybe he hit Locky in the head with an oar. Locky didn't like getting bopped on the head, so ..." she drew a line across her neck.

"Stan did think Locky was giving him the evil eye," I said. "Like Locky knew he had killed Stan's friend."

"See," Pat said. "There you go. Problem solved."

I shook my head and reached for a cookie. "I'd feel better if we found proof, outside of teeth marks, that Locky exists."

"What, like the proof Stan and Nevin found?" Pat asked drily.

I pointed the cookie at her. "And that's another thing. What's going on with the missing evidence? Did Nevin take it with him on the boat? Did he do something else with it? And if he did, then what?"

"I know. If Nevin's body hadn't shown up, I would be convinced that Nevin faked his death and ran off with it," Pat said.

"That was precisely what I was thinking when I talked with Stan," I said. "Where else would the notes be, except with Nevin? But now that we know Nevin didn't fake his death, it would seem he either took the notes on the boat with him—which, according to Stan, would be a major change in behavior—or Stan just hasn't been able to find them, maybe because of his head injury."

Pat frowned. "Neither sounds like a good explanation, if I'm honest."

I spread my hands out. "Well, what would be the third? Someone from the scientific community snuck in and stole them? The same person who killed Nevin?"

"A person wouldn't have left bite marks on the body, though," Pat said. Then, she blanched. "At least I hope not."

"I didn't see the body, but the way Wyle described them, I don't think they were human," I said. "It's possible someone killed Nevin, and then something else did the biting. Maybe whatever bit him decided the kill wasn't fresh enough to eat."

"That actually makes sense. It could apply to Locky, too," Pat theorized. "Maybe he didn't have anything to do with this death after all, and here he's getting blamed."

"I suppose there was a decent period of time during which someone could have snuck in and stolen the files," I said. "Stan was gone most of the day—first searching the lake, and then spending time at the hospital. If whoever killed Nevin took his hotel key, it would have been easy to sneak in and go through Nevin's room."

"That sounds like the most likely scenario," Pat said.

I made a face. "It does … logistically, at least. But what on Earth could those two have found that would be worth killing over?"

"I guess you're going to have to find those notes," Pat said.

I drummed my fingers on the table. "Yeah. In which case, maybe I'll find the killer, too."

"You better do it fast," Pat said. "Otherwise, poor Locky will probably end up being stalked by a lynch mob."

Chapter 8

I was in the middle of trying to get caught up on my tea orders (I was woefully behind, having been so distracted by Stan, Nevin, and Locky) when the doorbell rang.

Really hoping it wasn't a client wanting to know where her tea was, I hurried to the door.

It wasn't. Standing there was a woman I had never met, although she seemed familiar.

"Mrs. Kingsley?"

"Actually, it's 'Ms,'" I said. "Can I help you?"

She held out her hand. "I'm Deidre, Nevin's sister."

"Oh, of course." I should have recognized her, as the resemblance was obvious. Her hair was the same thin, sandy brown as her brother's, and cut in a short, no-nonsense bob. She also wore a similar style of glasses as he had on her round face. Even her clothes were a similar style—a button-down white shirt and khakis. "I'm so sorry for your loss."

"Thank you," she said. Her eyes were bloodshot, and her nose was red, but her demeanor was calm and collected. I wondered if she was still in a bit of shock.

"How can I help you?"

"I was hoping we could talk," she said. "I know I'm just dropping by unexpectedly, so if this isn't a good time, I understand."

"No, no, it's fine," I said, opening the door wider and sending a little mental message to my clients, hoping they wouldn't mind waiting a little longer for their tea. "Come on in."

I led her to the kitchen and offered her tea, which she refused. "Although I'm sure your tea is wonderful. I heard you run a store from your home," she said, looking around.

"Well, 'store' is probably a bit of an exaggeration," I said. "More like a tea business." I gestured to one of the kitchen chairs, and she gingerly sat down.

"I appreciate you seeing me," she said. "The police told me you were a witness in my brother's case."

"I don't know if I would call myself a 'witness'," I said. "The only thing I was a witness of was Stan nearly drowning the morning after your brother … went missing."

Her gaze was steady. "You mean, after he drowned."

"Yeah," I said sympathetically. "That's what I mean."

"But you met Nevin too, right?"

I nodded. "But it wasn't for very long. Just a few minutes while he was checking in to the inn."

She leaned forward slightly. "Would you mind telling me what happened there?"

"Sure," I said, and proceeded to give her a summary of our initial conversation at the Redemption Inn.

Deidre nodded. "Yes, that sounds like my brother."

She didn't say anything else, just stared out the window. I waited for her to say something, or to make some sort of move to leave, but she just sat there.

"Was there … something special you wanted to hear?" I asked.

She gave herself a quick shake and looked back at me. "Yes. No. I don't know. There's just … something about this that doesn't seem right."

She paused again, and I waited, wishing I had a cup of tea. Since Deidre had declined, I hadn't wanted to make myself one.

"He hasn't been himself lately," she said finally. "Something happened. I don't know what. But he was *happy*. He loved his job, and he loved teaching. And then," she shook her head angrily. "He got it in his head that he wanted to start this new … 'department.' And everything just went downhill from there."

"He was teaching cryptozoology?" I asked.

She huffed an exasperated sigh. "No! He was a zoologist! Just a plain, regular zoologist. I have no idea how he got into this whole cryptozoology nonsense. I think he took a class or read something. He was always studying, always learning. Like most professors, he loved being a student as much as he did teaching. But the next thing I know, he's babbling about wanting to be some sort of cryptozoologist and combine the para-normal with … well, I don't know what else. I know at one time, he visited the paranormal lab at Duke University, but I thought that was just some sort of lark. I had no idea he was taking any of this seriously."

I was surprised. "Oh, Stan made it sound like this was some-thing of a passion of Nevin's."

Deidre took off her glasses and rubbed her nose. "Obsession is more like it. But who knows what he told Stan? I don't even know where Stan came from. The first I heard of Stan and Nevin made it sound like they're best friends. Again, none of this is my brother. He's not someone who even has a lot of friends, much less to make one that quickly."

"So … you think something was wrong with Nevin?" I asked.

She sighed again and put her glasses back on. "I thought he was acting irrationally, but I figured it was some sort of midlife crisis and didn't say anything. It was only when he quit his job that I got concerned. I tried to get him to see a doctor, but he refused."

I could almost feel the pieces rearranging themselves in my head. Was this the reason the notes had gone missing? Because Nevin was no longer thinking straight? "Are you saying you don't think he was in his right mind?"

She gave me a look. "I KNOW he wasn't in his right mind. That's not even what concerns me."

"You think Nevin wasn't murdered," I said.

She glanced away, chewing on her lip. "I don't know what I think," she said. "But I'm almost positive he wasn't murdered. Who would kill him? And for what reason?"

"It's possible that someone in the scientific community might not want his research published."

Deidre laughed, but there was no humor behind it. "What, did Stan tell you that? No one cares about that research."

"Actually, both of them told me that," I said. "They talked about having irrefutable proof."

"Oh," She snorted. "There's no proof."

"How do you know?"

"Because I've seen it." She waved her hands in disgust. "It's ... nothing. A bunch of numbers that don't prove what they say it does."

I cocked my head. "How do you know that?"

She tilted her head, so she was looking at me over her glasses. "Because I'm a statistician. I understand numbers. The numbers they've collected are just ... meaningless." She sat back in her chair with a huff. "Trust me, anyone who knows anything is going to know it's all a load of crap."

"They said they found something more here, though," I said. "It's possible you haven't seen the real proof."

She rolled her eyes. "Possible, but unlikely."

I thought about how frantic Stan had been when he couldn't find the notes. Had Deidre truly seen all their data, or was there something more they had been holding back? They both already seemed paranoid. If Deidre had been badgering her brother to see a doctor, I wondered how much they would trust her with their greatest secrets.

Although, the fact that they WERE paranoid certainly made Deidre's claim that Nevin was losing his mind more credible. Not to mention the fact that Stan was still around, and Nevin wasn't. If someone killed Nevin because of the research, it seemed like Stan would have been targeted, too.

Unless Stan was next.

A chill ran over me. I really needed to get to the bottom of what was going on, and fast ... especially if Stan was in danger.

"When was the last time you spoke to your brother?"

She looked down at her khakis, her finger tracing one of the seams. "A couple of weeks ago. Since he quit, we ..." she swallowed hard. "We haven't spoken much, because it usually ended up a fight. In fact, the last time we talked, we fought, and he slammed the phone down on me." She blinked her eyes and glanced at me. "I don't know if I'll ever forgive myself."

My hand twitched to reach over to her, but I kept it where it was. "I'm sure he knew, deep down, that you loved him and were only trying to help."

"I hope so," she said, her voice glum.

"So, you don't have any ideas about his frame of mind more recently, then?"

She shook her head. "I wish I did, but no. I would assume it was the same, though. I don't know why it would have changed, and I imagine he would have reached out, if he had started to see reason again."

Based on what I had witnessed that first day, he still seemed to be all-in on his research, so I suspected she was right. "I know you said you don't know what you think, but you seem to … know your own mind," I said, thinking that was a nicer way of saying I thought she was opinionated. "If Nevin wasn't murdered, what's your best guess as to what happened to him?"

Deidre didn't answer, instead focusing on pulling on a thread on her khakis. "It was probably an accident," she said at last. "If I had to guess, he went out on that lake in the middle of the night, sure he was going to see something. And he probably did, whether his mind was starting to crack, and he was hallucinating, or it was simply wishful thinking. Or maybe he was on some sort of drugs or alcohol. Whatever it was, he was probably convinced he really did see something. I'm guessing in his excitement and confusion, he somehow fell out of the boat and drowned."

"What about the bite marks?"

"Happened after his body drifted to shore," she said dismissively. "Probably a bear or a mountain lion. Maybe even a wolf. I'm sure they're running tests right now to determine which animal did it."

What she said made sense. It wasn't a terrible theory. "Why wouldn't whatever animal bit him finish the job?"

"How should I know? I'm not the zoologist in the family," she snapped, her voice bitter. "Who knows why animals do the things they do. Maybe it got spooked, or something chased it away, or it couldn't drag the body out of the water for some reason. What does it matter? My brother is still dead, and for what? A stupid obsession."

Her voice cracked like she was about to cry, but her eyes remained dry. I wondered if she simply couldn't cry yet … the grief was too raw and new for tears.

"I'm truly sorry," I said. My hand itched again to reach over and squeeze hers, but there was a prickliness about her that made me think she didn't want to be touched.

"Thank you," she said stiffly, and she started to stand. "I've taken enough of your time."

I stood as well. "It's no problem. You haven't taken too much of my time at all. I'm not sure if I helped you much."

She pressed her lips together. "I don't know if anything can help." Her voice was hollow. "But you told me what I needed to know. I had assumed Nevin was still not in his right mind, and that was the cause of his death. Talking to you and the owner of that hotel confirmed it. I'm not happy to be right, but at least I know the truth."

Chapter 9

I was still mulling about my visit from Deidre when Wyle called.

"You'll never guess what those bite marks are from," he said.

"A bear?" I asked.

"No."

"A mountain lion?"

"Nope."

I paused. Not a bear or a mountain lion. "The way you described them before, it sounded like they were too big for a wolf … so I'm going to guess Locky."

"We have a winner."

I blinked. "What? Seriously? They're really from a Loch Ness Monster?'

"They're from a plesiosaur, actually."

"A dinosaur? But those are extinct."

"All but the one living in our lake, apparently," Wyle said. "At least according to the analysis."

"I can't believe it," I said, my brain whirling again. Deidre's visit had caused all the pieces to reshuffle, and now, the board had been shaken again.

"I know. It's tough to believe. I should note those results are preliminary—they haven't released their official report yet. They're still running tests, as something isn't adding up."

"Oh, you think?"

I could almost hear the smile in Wyle's voice. "Also, the drug and alcohol tests came back."

"And?"

"He tested positive for Rohypnol."

"Roofies?"

"That's what the lab said."

"Nevin tested positive for a date-rape drug?" I couldn't believe it. "What, was he out on a date with the plesiosaur, and it went horribly wrong?"

"If it helps, I've asked the lab to run the test again," Wyle said.

"How would he even get that drug?" I asked. "Did he stop somewhere before he went to the lake? Like maybe at a bar? Although I still don't see anyone drugging him on purpose. Whoever drugged him must have put the drug in the wrong drink."

"We're checking again," Wyle said. "We already made the rounds once, asking if he was in any of the bar owners' establishments the night he disappeared, but everyone said he wasn't."

"That is so weird," I said. "Although, if he had been on roofies, the drowning makes more sense. He would have been drowsy for sure, but other symptoms include loss of coordination and dizziness. That would have been a terrible combination for someone out in a boat, at night, by themselves. Quite honestly, it would have been a miracle if he hadn't drowned."

"Drugging him would have made him easier to drown, as well," Wyle said.

"That's true, but a roofie is an odd choice for a murderer, don't you think?"

"Maybe it was all the murderer had access to," Wyle suggested.

"Maybe," I said doubtfully, but I didn't buy it. I could sense I was missing something, something obvious, that would pull all the pieces together, but I just couldn't put my finger on it.

I hung up with Wyle and made myself some tea. Midnight joined me in the kitchen, his tail twitching as he sat next to his food dish.

"It's too early," I told him.

He flicked his tail.

"Fine," I said, picking up his dish. "I can at least do this right, even if I can't figure anything else out."

Midnight yawned.

"Alright, enough of the pity party. It's just I know I should be able to solve this. It's all right there."

He continued to stare at me, his green eyes unblinking, as I filled his food dish.

"So, on one hand, we have Stan, who seems convinced he has proof that's going to rock the scientific community. Maybe they really have stumbled onto something that would change everything. Like the Loch Ness Monster actually exists. It's possible."

I put the bowl down in front of Midnight, who began to eat.

"And if it is someone from the scientific community who is threatened by this discovery, or maybe even wants to steal it, then the roofie sort of makes sense. A lot of people in that community are associated with universities and colleges, and you can definitely find roofies there.

"On the other hand, we have Nevin's sister, who is convinced that Nevin is suffering some sort of mental breakdown, which is what led to his early demise. That doesn't explain the roofies in his system, although it also doesn't rule out that he could have accidentally ingested it. I suppose if he was having some sort of mental breakdown, it's possible he was associating with some questionable characters who could have slipped him the drug. But that seems like a long shot, too."

Midnight was still eating, but he flicked his tail.

"Yes, I know, neither of those explain the plesiosaur's bite." I leaned forward on the counter, propping my head with my hands. "What am I missing?"

Midnight didn't even flick his tail in response.

"You're no help," I grumbled.

He picked up his head, licked his whiskers, and sauntered out of the kitchen. I could almost hear him laughing at me.

Chapter 10

"Stan? Are you in there?"

I knocked again. Nancy had assured me that Stan was in his room, but there was no response to my knocks. I was starting to get a little worried. Had he had some sort of complication related to his concussion?

Or had Nevin's murderer come back for him after all?

"Stan? Are you okay? I need to know, or I'll have to get Nancy to let me in."

That got an answer. The door opened. "What do you want?"

It took me a moment to gather my thoughts to answer. Stan looked awful. His face was swollen, his hair greasy, and he smelled like perspiration and bad breath. "I ... uh, I was coming to check on you."

"Well, there. You checked. Goodbye." He started to close the door.

"Wait." I stuck half my body in the crack before he could shut it. "Stan, you don't look well. I need to do more than just see you. Can we chat for a few minutes? Maybe down in the lobby?"

He pressed his lips together, and I thought he was going to refuse. I didn't particularly want to sit in his hotel room with him, but if I couldn't get him downstairs, I would offer that next.

But then, he took a deep breath and sighed. "Fine," he said, running a hand through his hair. "I'll be down in a minute."

I was reluctant to leave, sure he was going to shut the door and never come down, but I also didn't have a good reason for sticking around.

"Nancy just took some snickerdoodle cookies out of the oven," I said, backing up so I was no longer blocking the door. "And I think she put a fresh pot of coffee on, as well."

He nodded and closed the door, and I headed to the lobby to find Nancy.

"I'm glad you're getting him down here," she called out from the kitchen as she gathered up the cookies and coffee. "He hasn't been down to breakfast since Nevin was found, and as far as I know, he hasn't been out for dinner, either."

"Does he have food in the room?"

She popped out of the kitchen with her hands full. "He did. He and Nevin used to eat lunch here all the time, so I'm assuming he had something. But he hasn't let me into the room to clean, either, so I can't be sure. Regardless, I don't think he's had a proper meal in a while."

"That would at least partially explain why he doesn't look good."

Her expression was full of compassion. "I'm sure it was hard on him, seeing his friend like that. Especially on top of his concussion."

"Yeah, I'm sure you're right," I said.

Nancy led me back to same table where I'd sat with Stan once before, leaving the coffee and cookies. I assured her I didn't need any tea this time.

It took about ten minutes for Stan to appear. I had nearly given up and was about to go back to his room and bang on his door, demanding to be let in, just as he arrived.

"I'm glad to see you," I said as he made his way silently to the table and sat down across from me. It looked like he had somewhat attempted to clean himself up. His face was washed, and he had changed his clothes. "I'm afraid your coffee might be cold," I said as he picked it up. "I thought you were going to be right down."

"I said, 'in a minute,'" he said bitterly, putting his cup back down. But his voice lacked the energy it had before. He seemed almost like a carbon copy of himself, flat and emotionless.

"I'm sorry about Nevin," I offered.

He nodded, staring at the table.

"I suppose it's a cold comfort, knowing you were right," I said. "Nevin really was bitten by a Loch Ness Monster."

"Plesiosaur," he corrected, still staring at the table.

"Ah, yes," I said. "Plesiosaur. And as a paleontologist, you would know that."

He didn't move. As far as I could tell, he wasn't even breathing.

"Did you know the results came back, proving it? Of course, everyone knows dinosaurs are extinct. But that doesn't mean someone like yourself, an expert in dinosaurs, couldn't recreate the bite of a plesiosaur. I have to commend you … you did a really good job of it. The initial lab results sure point to your fooling them. Of course, they're running more tests, so I'm guessing it's just a matter of time." I settled back in my seat as I crossed my legs.

Stan's throat worked as he swallowed. He looked genuinely confused for a moment before he continued.

"Why would I kill Nevin?" he asked, his voice scratchy. "He was my friend."

"That, I don't know," I said. "I would assume it had something to do with the missing notes, although Deidre thought whatever 'proof' you two discovered was actually nonsense."

At Deidre's name, Stan's head shot up. "Deidre is here? You talked to her?"

"Of course she's here. She's his brother."

"Do you think she's seen the notes?"

"I have no idea," I said. "I didn't ask her about that."

"Where is she? Maybe I can talk to her," he fretted.

I took a deep breath. "Stan," I said, as gently as I could. "You're in a lot of trouble here. You're going to be charged with murder."

Stan seemed to crumble in his seat at the words. "It wasn't supposed to be this way," he said.

Finally. Maybe we were getting somewhere. "What wasn't?"

"Any of this." He let out a heavy sigh. "When I first met Nevin and heard him talk about the new field of study he wanted to create, it was like a lightning bolt inside me. My entire life, I had been searching for something, but I couldn't put my finger on what. I knew I was supposed to do something great … to make my mark on the world … but I didn't know where to start or what direction to go. I went through a bunch of different majors before becoming a paleontologist, and I only stuck with that because it felt closest to what I was meant to be doing. At the time, I thought maybe I was supposed to discover a brand-new dinosaur, but it wasn't that at all. It was what Nevin was envisioning—starting para-cryptozoology as a new field of study. That was it.

"Of course, our university was too backwards to see Nevin's genius, so we had no choice but to quit. The plan was simple, but perfect. We would do our research and publish the findings, and once the scientific community saw our proof, they would have no choice but to start their own para-cryptozoology departments. We would have our pick as to where we wanted to go. Everyone would want us. We would be famous."

Stan had become more animated as he talked, his eyes lighting up with an unhealthy sheen. I found myself edging away from the table, trying to do it unobtrusively, so he wouldn't notice.

"So, what happened?"

Stan slumped over. "Nevin got cold feet. He kept talking about going back to our old jobs. He kept saying we could bring the research back and get our old jobs back. I kept telling him it wouldn't work … we quit! They weren't going to want us back. And even if we did go back, they still wouldn't start a para-cryptozoology department. But Nevin said it was baby steps—first, we start by getting our old jobs back and showing them our research. Then, we keep building on our credibility that way, until eventually, we'd start the para-cryptozoology department. He kept pointing out that our being unemployed would hurt our chances of getting our research published, and it would be better to eat a little crow and be affiliated with a university than it would be to keep trying to change the system from the outside."

"But you didn't want to do that," I said.

"No!" Stan banged on the table with his fist. "They screwed us! They laughed at us! How could we go back to that? I refused. It would be too humiliating to be back in the paleontology department, especially after everyone told us how crazy we were. I couldn't let them win."

"But Nevin wouldn't listen," I guessed.

"Worse! He went behind my back!" He banged his fist a second time on the table, rattling the cup of coffee and causing it to spill. His face and neck were turning a bright red. "He called his old boss and got his job back. He promised them our research, without my permission!"

"That's horrible," I said.

He pumped his head up and down. "Exactly. I was furious when he told me. He even had the gall to tell me he thought he had also gotten MY job back. I didn't want it! That wasn't what I was supposed to be doing. I was supposed to be known as one of the founders of para-cryptozoology. How dare he?"

"So, you had to kill him."

"How else was I supposed to stop him from stealing our research and giving it to the university?" He paused to take a breath, some of the anger draining from his face and neck. "I didn't want to, you understand. But I didn't see a way out. He was going to ruin both of us, not to mention all the work we had done."

"I thought Nevin was still going to publish it?"

"I'm sure that's what the dean told him, but it was all a lie. They would have buried it. I know it. They *laughed* at us. There was no way they would allow our research to see the light of day. It would make them look bad. So, this was the only way. The old Nevin would have known that. He would have appreciated what I did. And I had every intention of putting his name on it, too. He would still have gotten just as much credit."

I nodded, thinking that being dead, Nevin probably didn't care much about credit on a research paper. "So, what did you do?"

He paused, and I wondered if he was going to wise up and stop talking, but it was clear he wanted to tell someone. Maybe he needed to, in order to get it off his chest. "It made sense to do it on the lake. His body never should have come up. It should have worked out." His chest heaved. "I don't even understand why it did. And now, look. I'm ruined." He covered his face with his hands.

"But what actually happened?" I asked again gently.

He was quiet for so long, I thought he had changed his mind about confiding in me again, but then he started, his voice low. "The hardest part was getting him on the boat. I needed to figure out a way to incapacitate him enough to do so, but I also had to keep him conscious, so he could walk himself. I knew there was no way I could carry him. Nevin was never much of a drinker, just a beer or two, so I also knew I couldn't get him drunk. I had to use something else."

"You roofied him," I said.

He lowered his hands, his surprise genuine. "How did you know?"

"The tox screen came back."

He closed his eyes. "The body," he said in exasperation. "Why did it resurface?"

"How did you even get roofies, though?"

Another flush of red started to creep up his neck. "I confiscated some from one of my students last year. I was going to turn it over to the dean, but he ended up getting expelled a few days
later anyhow."

"And you had it with you?" I couldn't keep the disbelief from my voice.

"I had put them in the glove compartment of my car," he said. "I never took them out. Quite honestly, I had completely forgotten about it until I was trying to figure out what to use with Nevin."

I wasn't sure if I should believe him or not. It felt a little too coincidental that he just happened to have roofies in his glove compartment. On the other hand, it was such a ridiculous story, maybe it was true.

"I went to the library and looked up the symptoms and realized it would be like he was drunk. So, I slipped some into his beer that evening, and once it started to take effect, I convinced him we needed to go down to the boat. He didn't argue or fight me. It was actually easier than it should have been." He looked away from me, and for the first time, I saw a flash of something on his face. Was it remorse? Guilt? Grief? A combination? It was gone too quickly for me to put my finger on it. "Anyway, that was pretty much it."

"So, if you never thought the body would surface, why did you bother putting bite marks on it?"

He widened his eyes. "I didn't do anything with any bite marks. That was the plesiosaur."

I gave him a look.

"It was," he insisted, hitting his finger against the table. "I keep telling you, you have a plesiosaur in that lake. They're real."

"Does that mean you really did see Locky the next day?"

"Yes, I saw him. Do you think I wanted to almost drown? No. I was just out there pretending to look for Nevin. I had no plans to fall into the lake." He grimaced. "That was all the plesiosaur."

I sighed, wondering if he really believed what he was saying, or if he was trying to lay the groundwork for an insanity plea.

Chapter 11

"So, Stan did it after all," Pat said. We were standing in the Redemption Inn's breakfast room watching the police swarm around us. Nancy was behind the front desk, her hands on her hips and a frown on her lips—she was likely thinking about all the clean-up she was going to have to do in Stan and Nevin's rooms.

I called Pat after talking with Wyle. After Stan confessed, it was like something cracked inside him. He just sat there, his head bowed, completely still as I asked him if he was ready to turn himself in. "On one condition," he said, his words barely audible.

"What?"

His head shifted, barely, but enough for him to fix one blood-shot eye on me. "If you ever find those notes, you bring them to me."

Of course, I agreed.

"Yes," I answered Pat, coming back to present reality.

"Well, that at least means Locky is safe for now. Although he apparently still took a bite out of Nevin."

"I wouldn't go that far," I said.

Pat eyed me. "Stan confessed to murder. That's a lot worse than faking bite marks."

In my mind, I could still see Stan sitting in the chair like a broken doll. "His legacy is more important than his life," I said. "If everyone still thinks there's a plesiosaur in the lake that not only tried to eat Nevin, but went after Stan, too ... that makes Stan an instant celebrity."

Pat sighed. "Yeah, I guess you're right. Makes more sense than Locky wanting a snack."

I gave her a look. "I thought you didn't believe in Locky? You were more on the evil naiad side."

"That's true, but honestly, if I had to pick one, I would have to go with Locky. Locky seemed less ... violent."

"Even if it turned out Locky was real and tried to eat Nevin?"

"Yeah, but if that was the case, Nevin was already dead. Besides, until Nevin, I don't think Locky tried to eat anyone."

"Seeing as most of the bodies in Angel's Lake never resurface, we actually don't know that," I said.

"That's true," Pat said thoughtfully. "Locky could be quite the naughty boy."

I shook my head and watched one of the cops lug a box of files across the lobby. He was young, as in barely out of high school young, with long, gangly limbs and a way-too-thin body.

"Where do you think those notes are?" I asked Pat.

Pat shrugged. "If I had to guess, I would say probably in one of those file boxes." She angled her head toward the young cop.

"You think Stan just couldn't find them, after all his searching?"

"Based on what you said, he wasn't himself the past few days," Pat said. "My guess is, the guilt from killing his friend was eating him up inside. Plus, he was suffering from that concussion. I'm guessing he just missed the files."

I pondered that, picturing Stan's unwashed body and clothes and very unhealthy pallor. "Maybe. But I'm wondering if Nevin hid them."

"Why do you think that?"

"I'm not sure," I said. "I'm just thinking. Why would Nevin suddenly decide he wanted his old job back? When I saw him, he was clearly still all-in on this research. What could have changed his mind?"

"Maybe it was like his sister said, and he came to his senses," Pat offered. "He was experiencing some sort of mid-life crisis, but then, he woke up."

"Maybe," I said. "Or … maybe he realized the research was crap."

Pat did a double take, but before she could speak, I held my hand up.

"Hear me out," I said. "What if Nevin was going through the notes and came to the realization that what they'd discovered didn't mean what they thought it did? Worse, what if it was all worthless?"

"As in, unpublishable. They'd be laughed right out of the scientific community," Pat said.

"They'd never get jobs as professors, either," I said. "But Nevin can't convince Stan that it's worthless. So instead, he hides it, or maybe destroys it, so Stan can't run out and publish it behind his back, and then calls his old employer to see if they can get their jobs back."

"Nevin probably knew Stan would be upset at first, but if the research was 'missing' and Nevin was back at his old job, Stan would eventually come around," Pat continued the theory.

"Exactly. I'm sure he didn't expect Stan to be so upset, he would kill him," I said, slowly turning around the breakfast room. "While I think Nevin would have preferred to destroy it, the fact that he and Stan were always together probably made that difficult. So, I'm guessing he hid it somewhere."

Pat raised an eyebrow. "You think he hid it here?"

"Well, Nancy said they spent a lot of time in this room, so it makes sense," I said. "And Stan trashed Nevin's hotel room, so I really doubt it was there." My eyes kept flickering to the counter that stretched across one wall—the one Nancy used to display the breakfast items. I walked over and began examining it. It wasn't actually attached to the wall, but rather tightly pressed up against it. I went to the far end and shoved it back a little. It was heavy and made an awful groaning noise, but I managed to move it far enough to peer behind it.

And there it was—a file folder propped up behind it.

"You found it!" Pat squealed as I squeezed my arm into the small space to work it out.

"I did," I said as I emerged victorious. Pat came over to look over my shoulder as I immediately began leafing through the notes.

"What does this even mean?" she asked, her voice as bewildered as I felt.

"I don't know," I said. As far as I could tell, it was columns of numbers.

"Those look like dates," Pat said, pointing to one of the columns.

"Yeah, and these look like times, right? And are those temperature readings?"

"Maybe," Pat said. "But what's this?" She pointed to another column of numbers.

I shook my head. "I haven't a clue. Maybe they're measurements of current levels?"

Pat squinted her eyes as she looked closer. "Oh, that could be."

I continued leafing through the pages. "You think they were trying to prove that Locky existed based on temperature changes and current levels?"

"That's sort of what it looks like," Pat said. "Or maybe, it's more about the naiad. Bridget distinctly remembers a cold spot when she saw the eyes."

"It's not a terrible theory," I said slowly, my mind spinning in attempt to make sense of what I was looking at. "Something as big as a plesiosaur swimming around the lake would probably leave small changes in its wake. And if there was a naiad swimming around as well, I suppose it's possible. But I don't know." I closed the file and looked at Pat.

"I guess we'll never know, now," Pat said dejectedly.

"Probably not," I agreed. "My guess is, there was a problem with the data, which is why Nevin didn't want anyone else to see it. Whether it was because the data was bad or the theory itself was flawed will probably always be a mystery."

"Just like whether Locky is really in the lake," Pat said. "Unless, that is, another body resurfaces with teeth marks."

"Don't even say it," I said, pressing my hand to my chest and looking around as if we might be overheard. "That's the last thing we need here in Redemption."

"There really is never a dull moment in this town," Pat concurred.

Author's Note

Can't get enough of Charlie? I've got you covered. Start at the beginning with Book 1, *The Murder Before Christmas*.

A dead husband. A pregnant wife. A poisoned Christmas gift. Can Charlie discover the grinch who stole Christmas?

Grab your copy right here:

www.amazon.com/gp/product/B09H22K7LJ.

* * *

You can also check out exclusive bonus content for *Loch Ness Murder* here: mpwnovels.com/r/q/lochness-ebonus.

The bonus content reveals hints, clues, and sneak peeks you won't get just by reading the books, so you'll definitely want to take a look. You're going to discover a side of Redemption that is only available here.

* * *

If you enjoyed *Loch Ness Murder*, it would be wonderful if you would take a few minutes to leave a review and rating on Amazon:

amazon.com/dp/B0B9HTF57L/#customerReviews,

Goodreads:

goodreads.com/book/show/62564193-loch-ness-murder

or Bookbub:

bookbub.com/books/loch-ness-murder-charlie-kingsley-mysteries-by-michele-pariza-wacek

(Feel free to follow me on any of those platforms as well.) I thank you and other readers will thank you (as your reviews will help other readers find my books.)

The *Charlie Kingsley Mysteries* series is a spin-off from my award-winning *Secrets of Redemption* series. *Secrets of Redemption* is a little different from the *Charlie Kingsley Mysteries*, as it's more psychological suspense, but it's still clean like a cozy.

You can learn more about both series, including how they fit together, at MPWNovels.com, along with lots of other fun things such as short stories, deleted scenes, giveaways, recipes, puzzles and more.

I've also included a sneak peek of *The Murder Before Christmas*, just turn the page to get started.

Murder Before Christmas Chapter 1

"So, Courtney, is it?" I asked with what I hoped was a comforting and nonthreatening smile. I set the mug holding my newest tea blend I'd created for the Christmas season—a variety of fresh mint and a couple of other secret ingredients—down on the kitchen table. I called it "Candy Cane Concoctions", and hoped others would find it as soothing as it was refreshing. "What can I do for you?"

Courtney didn't look at me as she reached for her tea. She was young, younger than me, and extremely pretty, despite looking like something the cat dragged in. (And believe me, I know all about what cats can drag in. Midnight, my black cat, had presented me with more than my share of gifts over the years.) Courtney's long, wavy blonde hair was pulled back in a haphazard ponytail, and there were puffy, black circles under her china-blue eyes. She was also visibly pregnant.

"Well, Mrs. Kingsley," she began, but I quickly interrupted her.

"It's Miss, but please, call me Charlie." Yes, she was younger than me, but for goodness sake, not THAT much younger. Maybe it was time to start getting more serious about my morning makeup routine.

Her lips quirked up in a tiny smile that didn't quite reach her eyes. "Charlie, then. I was hoping you could make me a love potion."

I quickly dropped my gaze, busying myself by pushing the plate of frosted Christmas sugar cookies I had made earlier toward her, not wanting her to see my shock and sorrow. She was pregnant and wanted a love potion. This just couldn't be good.

"I don't actually do love potions," I said. "I make custom-blended teas and tinctures."

Her eyebrows knit together in confusion. "But people have been raving about how much you've helped them. Mrs. Witmore swears you cured her thyroid problems."

I tried not to sigh. "My teas and tinctures do have health benefits, that's true. Certain herbs and flowers can help with common ailments. In fact, for much of human civilization, there were no prescription drugs, so all they had to use were herbs and flowers. But I can't promise any cures."

"What about Ruthie?" Courtney asked. "She claims those heart tinctures you made are the reason Bob finally noticed her."

I gritted my teeth. When Ruthie's dad was recovering from a heart attack, I made a couple of teas and tinctures for him. Ruthie, who had a crush on her coworker Bob for years, was apparently so desperate for him to notice her that one day, she decided to bring one of my tinctures to work (I'm unclear which) and slip it into his drink. And apparently, shortly after that, Bob started up a conversation with her, and eventually asked her out on a date.

It didn't help matters that Jean, Ruthie's mother, had claimed my tinctures had reignited her and her husband's love life, which is probably how Ruthie got the idea to try them with Bob in the first place.

Needless to say, that was an unintended benefit.

"I didn't give Ruthie a love potion," I said. "I gave her dad some tinctures and teas to help his heart."

Courtney gazed at me with those clear-blue eyes, reminding me of a broken-down, worn-out doll. "Well, isn't that where love starts?"

"Maybe," I said. "But my intention was to heal her father's heart, not to make anyone fall in love with anyone else."

"But it worked," she said. "Can you just sell me whatever you gave her? I have money. I'll pay."

"It's not that simple," I said. "I really need to ask you some questions. It's always good to talk to your doctor, as well."

She bit her lip and dropped her gaze to the tea in her hands. She looked so lost and alone, I felt sorry for her.

"Why don't you tell me a little bit about who you want this love potion for?" I asked. "That would help me figure out how best to help you."

She didn't immediately answer, instead keeping her eyes down. Just as I was starting to think she wasn't going to say anything at all, she spoke. "It's for my husband," she said, her voice so low, it was nearly a whisper.

I could feel my heart sink to the floor. This was even more heartbreaking than I had imagined. "You think your husband fell out of love with you?"

"I know he has," she said. "He's having an affair."

"Oh Courtney," I sighed. "I'm so sorry to hear that."

She managed a tiny nod and picked up her tea to take a sip.

"Have you two talked about it?"

She shook her head quickly.

"Does he know you know?"

She shrugged.

"Maybe that's the place to start," I said, keeping my voice gentle. "Having a conversation."

"It won't help," she said, her voice still quiet.

"How do you know if you haven't tried?"

She didn't answer ... just stared into her tea.

"Have you thought about marriage counseling?"

"He won't go." Her voice was firm.

"Have you asked?"

"I know. He's said before he thinks therapy is a waste of money."

"Okay. But you have a baby on the way," I said. "You need to be able to talk through things. I understand it might be difficult to talk about something like *this*, but ..."

"He's in love with her." The words burst out of her as she raised her head. The expression on her face was so anguished that for a moment, it took my breath away.

"But how do you know if you haven't talked to him about it?"

"I just do," she said. "When you're married, you know these things. You can sense when your husband has fallen out of love with you. Hence, my need for a love potion. I need him to fall back in love with me. You can see how urgent this is." She gestured to her stomach. "In a few months, we're going to have a baby. I just *have* to get him to fall back in love with me."

Oh man, this was not going well. "I see why you would think that would be easier, but the problem is, there's no such thing as a love potion."

"Can you please just sell me what you made for Ruthie's dad? So I can at least try?"

"Whatever happened between Ruthie and Bob had nothing to do with one of my tinctures," I said flatly. "I don't want to give you false hope. I really think your best course of action is to have an open and honest conversation with him about the affair."

She was noticeably disappointed. It seemed to radiate out of every pore. I hated being the one to cause that, but I also wasn't going to sell her anything that could be misconstrued as a "love potion." Not only for her sake, but my own. The last thing I needed was lovesick women showing up at my door to buy something that didn't exist.

"Okay," she said quietly as she ducked her head so I couldn't quite see her face. "No love potion. How about the opposite?"

I looked at her in confusion. "The opposite?"

"Yes. Something that would kill him."

My mouth fell open. "Wha ... I'm sorry, could you repeat that?" I must have heard her wrong. She was still talking so quietly, not to mention hiding her face.

Courtney blinked and looked up at me. "I'm sorry?"

"I didn't hear what you said. Could you repeat it?"

"Oh. It was nothing." She offered an apologetic smile.

"No, really," I said. "I thought ..." I laughed a little self-consciously. "I thought you said you wanted something to kill your husband."

She blinked again. "Oh. Yeah. It was just a joke."

"A joke?"

"Yeah. I mean, you know. Sometimes married people want to kill each other. No big deal." Now it was her turn to let out a little twitter of laughter. "Have you ever been married?"

I shivered and put my hands around my mug to absorb the warmth. "No." Which was true. I had never been officially married, but that didn't mean my love life wasn't ... complicated.

Nor did it mean I didn't know exactly what she was talking about.

"Well, you know, sometimes married people can just get really angry with each other, and in the heat of the moment, even want to kill each other," she explained. "But they don't mean it. It's just because they love each other so much that sometimes that passion looks like something else. In the heat of the moment, in the middle of a fight, you can say all sorts of things you don't mean. But of course, they wouldn't *do* anything about it."

"Of course," I said. I decided not to mention that when she said it, she wasn't actually arguing with her husband. Nor did I bring up how perhaps she was protesting a bit too much.

I gave her a hard look as I sipped my tea.

She kept her gaze firmly on the table, refusing to meet my eyes. "Did I tell you how wonderful this blend is?" she asked. "It's so refreshing. Reminds me of a candy cane."

"Thanks. It's called 'Candy Cane Concoctions,' actually. I created it for the holidays," I said.

"It's wonderful." She took another hurried drink and put her mug down, tea sloshing over the side. "Are you selling it? Could I buy some?"

"Sure," I said, getting up from my chair. "Hang on a minute. I'll get you a bag."

She nodded as I left the kitchen to head upstairs to my office/work room. Although, to be fair, it was so small, it wasn't uncommon to find drying herbs or plants throughout the house.

I collected a bag and headed back to the kitchen. When I walked in, Courtney was standing up, fiddling with her purse. I instantly felt like something was off. Maybe it was the way she was standing or the bend of her neck, but she oozed guilt.

"Oh, there you are," she said, fishing out her wallet. "How much do I owe you?'

I told her, and she pulled out a wad of cash, handing me a twenty.

"I'll have to get you some change," I said.

"That's not necessary," she said, taking the bag. "You were so helpful to me, and besides, I need to get going."

"But this is way too much," I protested. "Just let me find my purse."

She waved me off as she left the kitchen and headed for the front door. "Nonsense. Truly, you were very helpful. No change is necessary." She jammed her arms into her coat, and without bothering to zip it up, opened the front door and headed out into the cold.

I closed the door after her, watching her through the window as she made her way down the driveway and into her car. She didn't seem very steady on her feet, and I wanted to make sure she got into her vehicle safely. After she drove off, I went back to the kitchen to look around.

Nothing appeared to be out of order. If she had been digging around looking for something (like something to kill her husband with), it wasn't obvious.

Still, I couldn't shake that uneasy feeling.

I went to the table to collect the dishes. Midnight strolled in as I was giving myself a pep talk.

"I'm sure she didn't mean it," I said to him. "She was probably just upset. I mean, she wasn't getting her love potion, and clearly, she was uncomfortable having a conversation with her husband. Although you'd think that would be a red flag."

Midnight sat down, his dark-green eyes studying me.

"Of course, that's hardly my business," I continued. "She's upset with him, and rightfully so. Who wouldn't be? Even if she wasn't actually joking in the moment, she was surely just letting off steam."

Midnight's tail twitched.

"Maybe this was even the first time she said it out loud," I said as I moved to the sink. "And now that she said it, she realized how awful it was. Of course she would never do anything like that." I turned to the cat. "Right?"

Midnight started cleaning himself.

"You're a lot of help," I muttered, turning back to the sink to finish the washing up.

As strange as that encounter was, it was likely the end of it. I hoped.

Murder Before Christmas Chapter 2

"Did you see the paper yet?"

"Good morning, Pat," I said into the phone. "So nice to hear from you. Oh, why yes, I did have a Merry Christmas. How was yours?"

"Go get your newspaper, and I'll be right over." There was a click, and the line went dead.

I replaced the receiver but didn't immediately move. There was a prickle of unease near the base of my skull. I had a sneaking suspicion I wasn't going to like what I saw in the newspaper.

Therefore, I took my time getting to it. I heated up water for a fresh pot of tea and put out some muffins I had baked the day before along with my new Christmas plates and napkins. Even though it was only me and Midnight, I still decorated the house—especially the kitchen. Normally full of sunflower decor, I had switched everything out for Christmas-themed items, complete with a small tree in the corner.

The whole Christmas season was bittersweet for me, but Christmas day was especially so. Christmas had always been my favorite holiday, but I missed seeing my niece Becca and my nephews, especially CB. My relationship with my sister Annabelle was still a little frosty. So, talking on the phone with them was easier.

After our call the day before, I'd spent a good chunk of the day baking before heading over to Nancy's house for Christmas dinner. Nancy, who owned the Redemption Inn, didn't have local family either, so we typically spent the holidays together at her place, where she could keep an eye on the inn.

The kitchen ready for Pat, I was about to fetch the paper when I decided I should maybe dress in something other than the old pair of grey sweatpants and sweatshirt I was wearing. I threw on a pair of jeans with one of my Christmas sweaters, red with a green tree in the center of it and ran a comb through my unruly brownish-blonde hair. It was somewhere between curly and frizzy, depending on the humidity, and today was definitely one of its wild days, so rather than deal with it, I pulled it back into a ponytail. I took a quick glance in the mirror, studying my eyes, which were an interesting mix of green, brown and gold, along with my full lips and narrow face, and wondered if I should dash on a bit of make up as well. I decided I didn't have enough time to mess around with it, and headed for the front door instead.

It was a cold, grey day outside. No snow yet, which was disappointing, as it would have been nice to have had a white Christmas. Still, it looked like it might start snowing any minute.

The paper was in the middle of the driveway, which meant I needed shoes. By the time I located my tennis shoes and laced them up, Pat had arrived and was heading up the driveway.

"Want to grab my newspaper while you're there?" I called out.

Her mouth dropped open. "You mean, you don't know yet?"

"It's Boxing Day, Pat," I said. "I didn't want to ruin Boxing Day."

"I don't even know what 'Boxing Day' means," Pat said as she detoured to scoop up my paper.

I shut the front door, knowing she would let herself in, and headed back to the kitchen to finish making the tea. I heard the front door open and close, and Pat appeared in the kitchen, her nose and cheeks bright red from the cold.

"I can't believe you didn't drop everything to get the paper," she grumbled, tossing it onto the table and snatching a muffin. Pat was a good decade or so older than me, and the best way to describe her was "round." She was plump, with a round face, round black-rimmed glasses, and short, no-nonsense brown hair that was turning grey. She had been one of my first customers, referred by Nancy, and had also become a good friend.

"Do you want to read it for yourself, or should I tell you?" she asked, taking a bite of the muffin. Like me, she also had on a Christmas sweater, except hers sported a family of snowmen holding song books and presumably caroling.

I brought the tea pot to the table and picked up the paper. "Neither," I said. "I told you, it's a holiday. Well, at least in Canada and the UK. We should be planning a shopping trip, not reading unpleasant happenings in the newspaper."

Pat rolled her eyes. "Trust me, you're going to want to see this," she said with her mouth full. "And, in case you didn't notice, we don't live in either Canada or the UK."

With a sigh, I slid the rubber band off and unrolled the paper.

A Murder Before Christmas, blared the newspaper. *Man Found Dead. Poisoned Present Suspected.*

"Poisoned *what*?" I muttered, reading the headline again. "Are they for real?"

"Don't worry about the headline," Pat said. "Just read the article."

I started to skim it.

Dennis Fallon, aged thirty-nine, was found dead in his home on Christmas Eve.

His wife, Courtney Fallon, aged twenty-five and six months pregnant, found him and called 9-1-1 ...

The words began to swim before my eyes. *Courtney Fallon ... six months pregnant.*

Had she told me her last name? I couldn't remember. But surely, this couldn't be the same woman.

An image of the haunted young woman who had sat in my kitchen a few weeks ago drinking my Candy Cane tea and asking for a potion to kill her husband appeared in my mind's eye.

It had to be someone else.

I quickly skimmed the article, searching for a photo of Dennis and his bride, when suddenly, my stomach twisted into a giant knot.

There, near the bottom. On their wedding day.

No question it was the same Courtney.

I looked up to see Pat pouring the tea. She handed me a mug. "You're going to need this. In fact, do you have anything stronger?"

I grasped the tea with limp fingers and collapsed into one of the chairs. "Pat, could I be responsible?"

Pat pulled out a chair and sat down across from me. "I don't know. Were you the one who sent him the poisoned brandy?"

"Poisoned bra ... *he was really poisoned*?"

"You didn't finish reading the article, did you?"

"No, I was just looking for a picture."

Pat shot me a look. "How many Courtneys do you think live in Redemption? Especially six-month pregnant ones?"

I picked up my tea to take a drink. It was hot and burned my tongue, but I drank it anyway. "I can't believe this is happening."

Pat reached for another muffin. "Oh, believe it. Do you want a muffin? Or should I find some Christmas cookies? I know you have some stashed in here somewhere ..."

Even though I had lost my appetite, I reached for a muffin. Maybe Pat had the right idea, and the sugar would help.

After Courtney left that day, I couldn't stop thinking about her. As much as I tried to write off what happened as frustration on her part—she didn't *really* want to kill her husband—I couldn't shake the feeling that something else was going on.

"Do you think I should tell someone?" I had asked Pat over tea and cookies.

Her expression was puzzled. "Who are you going to tell?"

"I don't know. The police?"

She blinked at me. "The police?"

"I mean, isn't that who you're supposed to tell if you have information about a crime?"

"Charlie, what exactly do you think you know? Someone came in here asking for a love potion because she's pregnant and her husband is cheating on her, and when it was clear she wasn't getting one, she asked for something else. You're talking about a pregnant woman who's upset because her husband is having an affair. There are probably a lot of women in that situation who have fantasized about killing their husband. Wouldn't YOU?"

I chewed on my lip. "I suppose."

What Pat had said made sense. The chances of her actually meaning it were pretty low.

And yet ...

Staring at Courtney's shy smile on the front page of the newspaper brought all my doubts back.

"So, do you want to tell me what happened, or do I need to read the article?"

Pat broke off a piece of muffin. "A package arrived for the mister on Christmas Eve. It appeared to be a present from one of his cousins, who just happened to be spending the holidays overseas. The note said something like 'Open me first for a little Christmas Eve cheer.' Inside was a bottle of his favorite brandy, so of course he had a little drink. Apparently, that's all it took."

"Where was Courtney when all this happened?"

"In the kitchen. She claimed they had decided to spend a quiet Christmas Eve at home, just the two of them, and she had spent the afternoon making a nice dinner. When he didn't show up, she went looking for him and found him lying on the floor of his study, dead."

My eyes widened. "Seriously?"

Pat nodded. "Yeah. Kind of weird, isn't it?"

"I'll say. Why would he be in his study drinking by himself when they were going to spend Christmas Eve together?"

"Good question."

"And she didn't hear him fall?" I continued. "You would think if a grown man collapsed, she would have heard it."

"Maybe she had Christmas music playing."

"Maybe." I frowned. "It still seems odd. So, after she found him, then what? Was she the one who called the cops?"

"Yep. And they pronounced him dead on the scene."

"This really does sound like she did it," I mused.

"Yeah, it does."

"Has she been arrested or charged or anything?"

"The paper didn't say," Pat said. "I would imagine they're keeping a close eye on her, though, at least."

"Maybe I should go talk to her," I said as I went back to studying Courtney's wedding photo. She looked impossibly young in a gorgeous wedding gown, her thick blonde hair piled on the top of her head. Her new husband was beaming at her.

"And say what? 'Hey, did you decide to poison your husband after all?'"

"Something like that, but maybe not quite as blunt." I couldn't tear my eyes away from her husband. Even if the news story hadn't mentioned his age, it was clear just in looking at him that he was much older than her, with his thinning hair and slight paunch.

But it was the look of love and adoration in his eyes that kept me glued to the page.

"I don't get it," I said.

"Get what?"

"Why he would cheat." I flipped the paper around to show Pat what I meant. "First of all, look at the age difference. She's young and pretty, and he's nearly middle age."

"So because he's middle aged, he wouldn't cheat?"

"No, but why *would* he? She appears to be a perfect trophy wife, if that's what he was looking for. But even more than that, look at how he's looking at her." I tapped the newspaper. "That doesn't look like a guy who doesn't love his wife."

Pat peered at the picture. "Maybe he fell out of love with her. We don't know when they got married."

"She's still pretty young. It couldn't have been that long ago."

"Maybe he's one of those guys who never wanted kids. And now that his wife is pregnant, he's lost interest."

"Possibly."

Pat glanced up at me, her eyes narrowing. "What are you saying? You don't think he was cheating on her?"

I thought about the visit with Courtney—how exhausted and depressed she had looked, and how sad she had been about her marriage. It sure didn't seem like she was acting; I had really felt her sincerity in thinking her husband was cheating on her.

"I'm not sure," I said. "I mean, Courtney sure seemed like she believed he was. But maybe she was wrong. Maybe he wasn't."

"How could she be wrong about something like that? How did she find out?"

"I don't know," I said. "I didn't ask. It didn't seem important at the time. But I do know they had never talked about it. So, it's possible she thought he was cheating for some reason, but he actually wasn't."

"Man, wouldn't it suck if she poisoned him over a misunderstanding?"

"What a nightmare." I sat back in my chair and stated twisting my ponytail around my hand. "I have to go see her. I mean, either he *was* cheating on her, which is unfortunate and kind of weird as she does seem to be a trophy wife, or he wasn't, but for some reason, she thought he was. Which is also weird."

"Or ..." Pat said, glancing at me out of the corner of her eye as she broke off another piece of muffin. "She made the whole cheating thing up."

I hadn't considered that theory. Was it possible she had invented the whole thing? I pictured her sitting at my kitchen table again, her beautiful blue eyes filled with sadness and grief. The idea she could have been faking caused a shiver to run up my spine.

I had to know the truth. Or at least, make an effort to find out what was going on. I ignored the little voice inside me that reminded me that this likely wasn't any of my business, and I had better things to do. I pushed myself out of my chair. "Want to come with me to visit the grieving widow?"

Pat tossed the last bite of muffin into her mouth. "Are you kidding? I wouldn't miss it for the world."

Want to keep reading? Grab your copy of **Murder Before Christmas** here:
amazon.com/gp/product/B09H22K7LJ.

More *Charlie Kingsley Mysteries:*
A Grave Error (a free prequel novella)
Ice Cold Murder (Book 2)
Murder Next Door (Book 3)
Murder Among Friends (Book 4)
The Murder of Sleepy Hollow (Book 5)
Red Hot Murder (Book 6)
A Wedding to Murder For (novella)
Loch Ness Murder (novella)

***Secrets of Redemption* series:**
It Began With a Lie (Book 1)
This Happened to Jessica (Book 2)
The Evil That Was Done (Book 3)
The Summoning (Book 4)
The Reckoning (Book 5)
The Girl Who Wasn't There (Book 6)
The Room at the Top of the Stairs (Book 7)
The Secret Diary of Helen Blackstone (free novella)

Standalone books:
Today I'll See Her (free novella or purchase with bonus content)
The Taking
The Third Nanny
Mirror Image
The Stolen Twin

About Michele

A USA Today Bestselling, award-winning author, Michele taught herself to read at 3 years old because she wanted to write stories so badly. It took some time (and some detours) but she does spend much of her time writing stories now. Mystery stories, to be exact. They're clean and twisty, and range from psychological thrillers to cozies, with a dash of romance and supernatural thrown into the mix. If that wasn't enough, she posts lots of fun things on her blog, including short stories, puzzles, recipes and more, at MPWNovels.com.

Michele grew up in Wisconsin, (hence why all her books take place there), and still visits regularly, but she herself escaped the cold and now lives in the mountains of Prescott, Arizona with her husband and southern squirrel hunter Cassie.

When she's not writing, she's usually reading, hanging out with her dog, or watching the Food Network and imagining she's an awesome cook. (Spoiler alert, she's not. Luckily for the whole family, Mr. PW is in charge of the cooking.)

Made in United States
North Haven, CT
21 March 2024

50292756R00055